BOOKS BY CLAIRE COOK

PRAISE FOR MUST LOVE DOGS

"This utterly charming novel by Cook is a fun read,
perfect for whiling away an afternoon on the beach."
—*Library Journal*

"Funny and pitch perfect."—*Chicago Tribune*

"Wildly witty"—*USA Today*

"Cook dishes up plenty of charm."
—*San Francisco Chronicle*

"A hoot"—*The Boston Globe*

"[A] laugh-out-loud novel . . . a light and lively read for
anyone who has ever tried to re-enter the dating scene
or tried to 'fix up' somebody else."—*Boston Herald*

"Reading *Must Love Dogs* is like having lunch with
your best friend—fun, breezy, and full of laughs."
—*Lorna Landvik*

"A hilariously original tale about dating and its place in
a modern woman's life."—*BookPage*

Marshbury Beach Books
Book Layout: The Book Designer
Author Photo: Stuart Wilson
Cover photo: Boryana Manzurova

Must Love Dogs: Bark & Roll Forever/Claire Cook
ISBN 978-1-942671-14-5
Ebook ISBN 978-1-942671-15-2

Must Love Dogs:
Bark & Roll Forever (#4)

Claire Cook

Marshbury Beach Books

One

John Anderson and I were actually going to move in together.

"Don't forget," I said from the passenger seat of his car. "We can't breathe a word about this to anyone in my family until it's too late for them to mess it up."

He nodded, shifted his hands on the steering wheel. "Got it."

We had a few other things to work out, too. For starters, I needed to stop thinking of him as John Anderson. But referring to him by his first name only, even to myself, somehow seemed overly optimistic. Like admitting out loud that I hoped he'd be the only John for me, forever and ever. I was pretty sure that I was afraid I might jinx the whole thing if I dropped the Anderson.

I flashed back to visiting my grandparents when my siblings and I were still kids. In the middle of a rowdy game of hide-and-seek in the alley behind my father's parents' triple-decker, my grandfather appeared on the third floor porch and looked out over the petunias that tumbled over the edges of the window boxes. "And what are you little hellions looking so happy about down there?" he said, the lilt of Ireland in his voice. "Don't you know that happy is for the next life?"

I didn't want to wait for the next life for happy. "John, John, John," I whispered.

"What'd I do?" John Anderson said. John.

"Nothing," I said. "At least not yet."

"Good to hear." He took his eyes off the road just long enough to give me a smile. My heart did the little flip flop thing it did when we made eye contact.

We also had to get his Boston condo rented, sell my Marshbury ranchburger, and find a house to buy together. There would be three of us, since John-not-Anderson and his dog Horatio were a package deal. Horatio was the product of a dalliance between a Yorkie who'd briefly lived in John's building and a runaway greyhound, though he'd somehow come out looking like a scruffy dachshund. I'd worked hard on my relationship with Horatio, and though he wasn't exactly my new best four-legged friend, he'd gone from hating my guts to finally accepting the fact that I wasn't going anywhere. At least I hoped I wasn't.

"So," I said. "Shall we hit one more open house before we brave Sunday dinner with my family?"

John checked his dashboard clock. "Do you think we have enough time?"

"Sure. I'm always late. That's why they make me bring dessert. If I showed up on time for a change, my family would totally know something was up." I turned to make sure the two bakery boxes we'd picked up at Morning Glories hadn't skidded off John's backseat. The chocolate chip hazelnut cookies would probably be okay a little crumbly, but the fresh fruit tart might not survive a fall.

John shrugged. "Okay, then. Maybe we'll get lucky this time. I didn't feel any chemistry at all with those first five houses."

"Ha," I said. "You make it sound like we're looking for a house to date."

"More like a long-term commitment." John put on his blinker and pulled into the beach parking lot, which was almost full on this perfect fall day.

We found a parking spot, climbed out of the car to stretch our legs and gulp down a breath of salt air. Then we both leaned back against his car and pulled up the lists of open houses we'd made on our phones.

"How about this one?" John said. "*Won't last long. Spacious home with peek-through water views. Four bedrooms, three baths, central heat and air, certified ghost-free.*"

"Ghost-free is good," I said. "And you don't always find central air in New England either, especially in older houses. Ooh, listen to this one: *I have new paint and appliances, hardwood floors, open floor plan, dual sinks in master, attached two-car garage. Wow, and get this—a huge dick for entertaining."*

I held up my phone so John could see the listing. "Great typo," he said. "There'll be a line a mile long for that open house."

"Yeah, maybe we should skip that one in the interests of time." I batted my eyelashes at him. "Especially since we've already got the perfect deck for entertaining."

"Why, thank you, ma'am." He leaned in for a kiss.

I was just about to suggest we blow off both the house hunt and Sunday dinner with my family and head back to my place when a text jingled in to my phone.

"Damn," I said. "How to ruin a moment."

"Ah, technology," John said. "Can't kiss with it, can't live without it."

I started looking around for my phone, realized it was still in my hand.

The text was from my older sister Carol's seventeen-year-old daughter, Siobhan.

Hey where r u babe? my fam only gone couple hrs xo

I shook my head, thought for a moment, typed a reply.

Thanks for the invite. I'll be right there! xo Aunt Sarah

"So in a nutshell," John said as we climbed back into his car. "Your niece accidentally texted you instead of her boyfriend, and you've just ruined her home-alone rendezvous because now she'll be too worried about you showing up to enjoy it?"

"Exactly," I said. "Wow, you're really catching on."

John turned the key in the ignition. "So that means we don't have to actually go over there, right?"

"Relax. Of course we don't have to go over there. But Siobhan doesn't know that, which keeps the boyfriend out of her house, and you and I still get to go to one more open house. It was actually a fairly genius move on my part, if I do say so myself."

John's Heath Bar eyes, a circle of toffee surrounded by a darker ring of chocolate brown, looked at me with concern. "On some level, do you think she was trying to get caught?"

I reached for my seatbelt. "I don't think so. I think she's being seventeen. There aren't necessarily a lot of levels at that age—mostly just a whole bunch of raging hormones."

"And the ever-present, though not necessarily realistic, hope that your teenage deck will finally get to do some entertaining."

I laughed, tried not to remember my own painful teenage years, which mostly consisted of having mad crushes on guys who had absolutely no interest in me. And completely ignoring the ones who were interested, because I mean, seriously, what was their *problem*?

John turned the key in the ignition. "And now you'll tell your sister Carol about the text so she can take it from here?"

I shivered at the thought. "Oh, God, I hope not."

. . . . .

I played copilot, giving John directions as he drove. Since the open house we'd decided on was in Marshbury, I didn't even need to type the address into his GPS. I'd spent most of my life here, so I could probably draw a street map of the entire town from memory if I had to.

It was the perfect little beach town. Small enough but not too small, tree-lined streets, wide sidewalks. Marshbury, Massachusetts had all the charm of that old TV show, *Mayberry RFD*, but with the added perks of great restaurants and trendy shops, all conveniently tucked in next to an ever-changing and endlessly spectacular ocean.

We'd been house hunting for over a month now. John was making the big sacrifice by moving out of his Boston condo, which was close to his job, because I didn't think I could survive, let alone thrive, living in the city and commuting to my Marshbury teaching job at Bayberry Preschool.

John ran the accounting department at a digital gaming company called Necrogamiac. He didn't think he could handle the hellish daily commute from the 'burbs to the city, so he'd talked his boss into letting him work remote most days once we'd found a place.

John wasn't planning to sell his condo. Instead, he'd found a short-term executive rental company, his idea being that we could occasionally use the condo ourselves between tenants as an urban getaway.

In my least secure moments, I wondered if John was keeping his condo as backup, just in case things didn't work out between us.

I hit the button that turned on John's radio. Gloria Gaynor was belting out "I Will Survive." This seemed like a decent oldies omen, maybe not quite as good as The Beatles singing "We Can Work It Out," but a helluva lot better, as far as fortune telling via radio went, than tuning in to have Elvis serenade us with "Heartbreak Hotel."

John and I tilted our heads toward each other and sang the last chorus along with Gloria. Then he reached over and turned down the radio. "We'll get through this. We just have to take it one move at a time so it doesn't feel so overwhelming."

I sighed. "But they're all connected. You know, like dominoes. If you let that company rent your condo and you and Horatio move in with me, it'll be hard to put my house on the market because we'll be crammed in there like sardines. And if we both pack up most of our stuff and move it all into a storage unit, we won't be able to find the things we need when we need them. And what if we rent your place and sell mine, and then we can't find a house we both like? And what if my house doesn't sell? And . . ."

A wind-battered bouquet of blue and white helium balloons attached to an open house sign greeted us at the corner of the street.

John put on his blinker, made the turn, found a space in a line of cars that edged one side of the road.

When I joined him on the tree-shaded sidewalk, John was writing the address of the open house at the top of a fresh page on his house-hunting clipboard. He devoted a page to each house we visited, a vertical line dividing the page exactly in half, pros on the left side, cons on the right. This kind of systematic dorkiness was part of John's charm. And besides, who was I to say anything, since I'd used the exact same system when my family had pushed me, kicking and screaming, back out into the dating world after my divorce.

Which had led me to John Anderson.

John.

He rested the hand not holding the clipboard on my shoulder. "It'll all work out, Sarah. Worst case scenario, maybe your dad will let us camp out with him for a month or two."

"Ha," I said. "That's really funny."

Two

"Well, it did have a porch," John said.

John and I were in agreement that a front porch big enough to hold some chairs and a porch swing was an absolute must for our new house.

"Take a right at the next corner, then a left," I said. "It's a short cut. Sure, it had a decent porch, but that was pretty much all it had. I mean, it *was* a Victorian, but the cramped kind, like a wannabe version of my family's house. All those low ceilings and little rooms . . ."

John shook his head. "What a shame the original floors had been replaced. The old crown molding and wainscoting were long gone, too."

"Yeah, and not that watching HGTV makes me an expert," I said, "but what was there looked like off-the-rack trim from Home Depot to me."

"Based on my own HGTV-viewing experience, I concur. So, essentially, we'd have all the issues of an old house, but none of the charm. I say we rule it out."

"Done." I reached for the clipboard, drew a big X across the page. This triggered another quick flashback to the pages I'd kept during my dating days: Drawing an X through the guy who was looking for a relationship one day a month, no strings, no commitments. And another X through Lennie, whose extreme neediness left me gasping for air without even meeting him. Another X through the guy looking for a plus-sized Woman, whom I'd briefly considered partly because I liked the way he capitalized Woman, but mostly because I could eat a lot. And one through Ray, the former almost hockey star I'd almost slept with. And belatedly, a great big X through Bob, a former student's father I shouldn't have slept with.

I took a long, deep centering breath, hoping to quell my residual self-destructive impulses. I'd found that needle in a haystack, a nice, normal guy who actually loved me. And I loved him. We'd buy a house. We'd build a life together. If the world threw us a curveball or two along the way—and I was old enough to know that it would—we'd stick together and we'd be okay.

At least theoretically.

We swung by my house to pick up Horatio. A quick bathroom break all around and then the three of us jumped into the car. Five minutes later we pulled into the driveway of the house I grew up in, the crushed mussel shell driveway making a satisfying *crunch* under John's tires.

The thing about having a big family is that when everybody shows up for Sunday dinner, it turns into a crowd. We parked behind all the other cars and minivans and SUVs like a caboose.

A gathering of sugar maples had dropped enough leaves to create a patchwork of reds and yellows and oranges on the front lawn. Every year a solitary Japanese maple closer to the house lost its feathery red leaves, starting at the top and working its way down to the bottom as if it were going bald. Scraggly burgundy chrysanthemums, leftovers that had been coming back every year since the last time someone had thought to plant fresh ones, were doing their best to bloom in between the overgrown yews and rhododendrons and azaleas edging the fieldstone foundation.

An old metal swing hung from the beadboard-covered porch ceiling by four slightly rusted metal chains. The swing, painted black to match the shutters on the white house, had been there for as long as I could remember. It was big enough to hold three adults, or as many kids as could pile on.

"Now *that's* a porch," John said.

"Agreed," I said.

Halfway up the front steps, Horatio started barking like a maniac.

John bent down, scratched him behind the ears. "What's up, buddy?"

I shifted the bakery boxes in my arms. "He probably just smells my family."

Horatio scurried up the rest of the steps, growled, attempted to shove his nose between the porch floorboards. When that didn't work, he barked some more while he tried to claw a larger opening.

"Chipmunks?" John said.

I shrugged, gave the tarnished brass doorknocker the obligatory thunk, opened the door.

Mother Teresa, my brother Michael's humongous St. Bernard, lumbered around the corner to greet us, my two youngest nieces Maeve and Sydney hot on her trail. Mother Teresa stopped a few feet away from Horatio, tail wagging, and lowered her body into the downward dog position that had inspired the yoga pose. Horatio, several feet shorter and about a hundred pounds lighter, did the same thing.

Maeve and Sydney giggled, then stretched into their own versions of downward dog.

John leaned over and unhooked Horatio's leash.

"And they're off," I yelled as kids and canines raced down the long center hallway.

. . . . .

There were so many of us that it was impossible to see who was there and who wasn't until we were seated. All six grown Hurlihy kids and their significant others squished in elbow to elbow around the long dining room table, made longer by yanking both sides in opposite directions and pulling up two leaves hidden underneath.

The next Hurlihy generation was arranged around an assortment of card tables that abutted one end of the dining room table to form a T. Dining room chairs mingled randomly with kitchen chairs, folding chairs, two old wooden highchairs with the trays removed, and a couple of backless wooden stools.

"Hey," I said. "Where's Dad?"

"Hot date?" my brother Michael said.

"Five will get you ten," my brother Billy Jr. said.

Whoever didn't have other plans showed up for Sunday dinner at our Dad's house, in varying configurations, whenever it worked out. Sometimes we all brought food, sometimes we ordered takeout. If our father wasn't there, we ate without him.

Billy Jr. rested his clasped hands on the table and bowed his head. "Rub-a-dub-dub, thanks for the grub, amen."

"Yay, God," we all yelled. This passed for grace in our family.

Everybody held up their glasses—wine for the adults, milk for the kids.

"May you live as long as you want and never want as long as you live," Billy Jr. said.

"May you be in heaven a full half hour before the devil knows you're dead," I said.

"Sláinte!" we roared, which is the Irish equivalent of cheers, though it actually means *health* and sounds like slurring *it's a lawn chair* really fast. We clanked glasses all around.

"Dad does it better," my sister Christine said.

"True," my brother Johnny said. "But you have to admit, when we fly solo it goes faster. Dad would still be reciting poetry for the next twenty minutes."

"Hail Mary, full of grapes, the Lord is a tree," my older sister Carol's daughter Maeve yelled from the card table section.

"Maeve," Carol said.

"I thought it was actually a damn good toast for a three-year-old," I said.

"Damn!" my sister Christine's daughter Sydney yelled.

"Thanks for that," Christine said.

A glass of milk tipped over, causing a minor flood in the kiddie section. Christine jumped up, grabbed a pile of paper napkins from the sideboard.

"Well, that didn't take long," Carol said. "Now I get why Mom and Dad didn't let us have drinks at the table."

"You know," I said, "I still can't eat and drink at the same time. I have to take shifts."

"Odd," Michael said. "Your mouth is certainly big enough to do both at once."

"Shut up," I said.

"No, you shut up," he said. My siblings and I had a slight tendency to revert to our childhood selves as soon as we got together.

"Where's Siobhan?" Michael's wife Phoebe said, possibly to make us stop.

"She has a big history test tomorrow," Carol's husband Dennis said, "so we let her stay home to study."

John and I made eye contact, looked away. I took a long sip of wine.

Carol served herself some lasagna, passed it to the next person. "So," she said. "How's the house hunting going?"

I looked around casually. "Who's house hunting?"

"Good try," Carol said. "But we've known about it for weeks. One of my clients saw you at an open house over on Wash Ashore Drive." My sister Carol was the family know-it-all. That she had her own business as an event planner and practically everyone in Marshbury had worked with her at one time or another only added to her power.

"Don't even think about buying that house," Johnny said. "The fire department will be rescuing you in a rowboat as soon as the first hurricane hits."

"Actually," Michael said, "I think they use amphibious vehicles now. The National Guard brings them in."

"So what we've been thinking," Billy Jr. said, "is that maybe you guys should move in with Dad."

"Ohmigod," I said. "You've been talking about me behind my back."

"Like that's something new," Christine said.

"It's a beautiful house," Billy Jr.'s wife Moira said.

"Dad's not getting any younger," Michael said. "And it wouldn't hurt to have somebody in here keeping an eye on him."

"Right," I said. "And all of you would still march right in like you owned the place whenever you felt like it."

"Look on the bright side," Carol said. "If you already lived here, at least you'd be on time for Sunday dinner for a change."

"No way," I said. "Never. Not going to happen. And whatever you do, do not, I repeat, *do not*, mention a word about this to Dad."

"Do not mention a word about what to Dad?" our father said from the doorway.

I glared at my siblings. "Nothing," I said. "We were just talking about what to get you for Christmas this year."

"Don't let me stop you," our dad said as he strolled toward his seat at the head of the table, which we always left empty for him just in case. "But you kiddos are all wet if you're contemplating buying me anything other than that 72-inch flat screen TV and the recliner with the dual beverage holders. A minibar would come in handy, too, should you happen to be rolling in dough this year."

He grabbed a bottle of wine off the table, winked at his grandkids before he sat down. "I know you kiddos tried your darndest to win them for me in that Upgrade Your Dad Sweepstakes, but just for the record, close only counts in horseshoes and the foxtrot."

Three

Mother Teresa and Horatio had inspired me to try some yoga in my classroom.

"Just follow my lead," I said to my new assistant Polly. "And try not to hurt yourself."

I'd hired Polly right before the school year started when Kate Stone, my bitch of a boss, had pulled a last-minute switcheroo, sending June, the assistant I'd spent an entire year training, off to work with the new teacher she'd hired.

I waited until Polly finished placing a laminated nametag on the floor in front of each of the evenly spaced dots on our classroom circle. The circle is the heart of the classroom, but getting a bevy of three-, four- and five-year-olds to assemble there takes some planning.

"Circle time," I sang.

During the first week of school, each of the children had chosen a sticker for their nametag. So four-year-old Julian would see his name in block letters, along with the picture of a dump truck he had chosen himself. Finding his place was a complicated process of discovering his dump truck, "reading" his name, locating the adjacent dot, and successfully bringing his butt in for a landing on it.

In a good year, the nametags would be removed sometime during October, and even the youngest children would be able to find their places without them. It was October and we were close, but we weren't quite there yet.

"Dumb fuck," three-year-old Depp said as he walked by Julian's nametag.

"I'm not a dumb fuck," five-year-old Celine said. "You're a dumb fuck."

A mispronunciation like that could spread like wildfire, and when it showed up again at dinnertime, my phone would be ringing off the hook with irate parents. "Dump truck," I enunciated carefully. "Dumppp. Trrr-uck."

"I knew we should have ditched that sticker," I whispered to Polly.

"Where's my titties?" three-year-old Morgan said as she stomped around the circle.

"Kitties," I said. "Kuh, kuh, kitties."

"Ohmigod," Polly whispered. "How do you keep a straight face? They are so adorable."

"You might find them slightly less adorable if their parents had *your* phone number," I whispered back.

Eventually, all the kids were evenly spaced around the circle. Polly put the nametags away and joined them. I grabbed the yoga cards I'd stayed up way too late making and took my own place.

I made a peace sign, our classroom signal to stop talking, stop everything.

Polly and the kids made peace signs back at me, some of the three-year-olds using their other hands to wrestle their stubby fingers into place.

I put the soles of my feet together.

Polly and company put the soles of their feet together.

I took a loud breath in as I reached my hands up over my head.

They imitated me with monkey-see-monkey-do precision.

I blew out a deep breath as I stretched forward, reaching my hands toward the center of the circle until they touched the floor. Everybody stayed with me.

I sat up straight again, my exaggerated breath signaling the move. Then I reached for the card with a picture of a butterfly on it. I held it out facing the kids and made a long left-to-right swoop with it so they could all get a good look. I put the card down, face up, held my feet together with both hands, and bounced my knees up and down.

A circle's worth of pretend butterflies flapped their wings.

I found the cat card, gave it a swoop, put it down. I got on my hands and knees, waited for everybody to catch up with me.

"Meow," I said as I arched my back and lifted my head up until I was looking at the ceiling.

"Meow," a chorus of copycats answered me.

"Purr," I said as I rounded my back and dropped my head down to look at the floor.

"Purr."

We stayed on our hands and knees while I found the dog card, circled it around with one hand to make sure they all saw it.

"Woof, woof, woof," I said. I tucked my toes under. Then I lifted my hips and buttocks up in the air until my arms and legs were straight and I was in a downward dog position.

"Woof, woof, woof," the kids parroted as they lifted their hindquarters.

And the room erupted in a cacophony of preschool farts.

. . . . .

"It's all that sugary breakfast cereal," Lorna said over lunch in the teachers' room. Lorna was one of my favorite teaching colleagues and partners in crime. "It causes a fartfest every time they go upside down."

"Or hug their knees into their chests," Gloria said. Gloria was our other favorite teacher and accomplice. "I'm sure you handled it beautifully. You always do, honey."

"I don't know about that," I said. "Nose-picking is so much easier. You just hand them a tissue. So once the hilarity died down, I explained that it was the sound of air leaving our bodies, and we all needed to remember to say 'excuse me' when it happened. Anyway, Polly got the worst of it. Griffin Fanning is not quite as toilet-trained as his parents led us to believe he was."

Assistants, at least at Bayberry, had to do most of the daily cleaning as well as the mopping up of assorted bodily fluids. After the three- and four-year-olds went home or to Bayberry childcare just before lunchtime, the assistants usually ate lunch in the classroom with the five-year-olds so the teachers could take a break. But the teachers were ultimately responsible for anything that went wrong, and also had to deal with the parents, which pretty much balanced things out.

I sighed. "And we also had a dumb fuck *and* a tittie. That's a lot for one morning."

"Look on the bright side, sweetie," Gloria said. "Now that they're banned from the premises because of allergies, at least we don't have to deal with the younger kids cracking up the older kids by saying penis instead of peanuts."

"Good point," I said. "That one was practically an epidemic."

"Well," Lorna said. "All I had this morning was a three-year-old announcing that he wanted mobster for his snack. I finally figured out he meant lobster. Not that our precious little students are entitled or anything."

"How did you handle it?" Gloria asked.

Lorna smiled. "I gave him a Dixie cup's worth of Goldfish and told him they were cousins."

"Good thinking," I said.

"Thanks." Lorna helped herself to one of my baby carrots. "And your ex-husband's twins are completely out of control, if that makes you feel any better."

I closed my eyes and covered my ears. "Please don't."

When I was married to my former husband Kevin, he was never quite ready to have kids. I was almost ready, then ready, then more than ready. Just when I was verging on too late, Kevin left me for someone named Nikki, chatty as hell and ten years younger than me. And already pregnant with the kids he hadn't wanted with me. Twins, no less.

Like that wasn't enough, Kevin and Nikki had not only enrolled their offspring, one named after each of them, at Bayberry, but they'd requested me as the teacher. I'd managed to nix the classroom placement, but my wasband's kids were still in the school, and Lorna was their teacher.

When I opened my eyes, Lorna and Gloria were staring at me.

"You don't still have a thing for him, do you?" Lorna asked.

Gloria put a hand on Lorna's forearm. "Leave her alone. If she has a thing for her ex, it's not our business, sweetie."

"Give me a break," I said. "I do not, I repeat, *do not*, have a thing for my ex-husband. In fact, my goal is to get through the entire school year without once running into him."

"Good luck with that," Lorna said.

The teachers' room door squeaked open. Ethan, the new teacher, resident school hunk, and our bitch of a boss's godson, took a step in and stopped.

"Am I interrupting anything?" he said. His sun-streaked surfer boy hair sparkled under the overhead fluorescents.

"Not at all," Lorna said. "We were just discussing the latest preschool methodology."

"Don't fall for it," I said. "We were actually having a riveting conversation about farting."

"And Sarah's ex-husband," Gloria said.

"Your ex-husband was a farter?" Ethan said. "How fascinating."

I shook my head, pushed myself up to a standing position. "Here, you can have my seat. I think I've had all the lunch I can take."

"Wuss," Lorna said.

Of course, my life being my life, as soon as I walked out of the teachers' room and hung a left, I practically ran right into my ex-husband.

"Avert your eyes," I said. "Or you'll turn to salt. Or die. Or something fun."

Kevin laughed as if I were kidding, fell into step beside me. He smelled exactly the same, like coffee and cinnamon Altoids and some kind of musky male scent that was just him.

"Nice sweater," he said. "Blue's still a great color on you."

I shook my head, picked up my pace.

He picked up his.

I stopped, turned around, pointed. "Childcare's that way."

"So," he said. "The twins are doing really well so far. At least I think they are. Their teacher hasn't mentioned anything to you about it, has she?"

"Did you actually just fake compliment me to get the scoop on how your kids are doing?" I meant to whisper it, but it came out more like a hiss.

Kate Stone, my bitch of a boss, appeared out of nowhere, wearing Birkenstocks and a boysenberry-colored Batik tunic over an ankle-length black skirt. "Everything okay here, Sarah?"

"Perfect timing," I said. "One of the parents was just looking for you. He's hoping you can give him some strategies for dealing with his separation anxiety."

Four

John was spending the week at his condo so that he could get ahead on his work. When and if we actually found a house and could finally spring into action, this would give him some wiggle room. Staying in Boston for the week also meant that Horatio could go to his puppy playcare, which he loved.

When my cell rang, I knew it was John before I even looked at his name on the screen.

"Hey." I leaned back against my headboard, slid my bare feet under the covers, tucked a pillow behind my head. "Good day?"

"Not bad at all. I got a lot done, had a one-on-one with my boss, then lunch with one of the marketing guys. You know, business as usual. How 'bout yours?"

"Hmm, let's see," I said. "I did some yoga with the kids, which turned into a preschool fartathon. The vocabulary words of the day were dumb fuck and titties. And my ex managed to cross paths with me, but I sent him to the principal's office, so it all worked out. You know, business as usual."

"Wow," John said. "It never ceases to amaze me how closely our workdays resemble each other."

"Ha," I said. "Oh, and I swung by to see Siobhan after school today, just like I said I would. She wasn't there, but I told Carol to tell her that her favorite aunt needed some hangout time and to call me."

"Did you mention the errant text to Carol?"

"We've already been over that. What would it accomplish, besides making my niece hate my guts? And it's not like I *lied* to Carol. When it comes to sins, there's a huge difference between omission and commission."

"How so?"

I sighed. "Never mind. I guess it's a brought-up-Catholic thing."

"Couldn't you ask Carol to keep you out of it? Just give her a heads up so that she can keep a closer watch on Siobhan?"

"Right," I said. "Carol would throw me under the bus the second Siobhan started denying it. No, the best thing to do is to spend some one-on-one time with Siobhan, find out what the deal is with the boyfriend, and then offer her the benefit of my wisdom and experience, as well as whatever support she needs."

"Okay then," John said neutrally. I knew he didn't agree with me. He knew it wasn't really his business.

I held my phone with my chin while I pulled the covers up. "So," I said casually. "Not pregnant."

There was a long moment of silence. "Did you think we—you—were?" John finally said.

Clearly we had some pronoun work to do. I tended to circumnavigate the pronoun decision altogether by not using one, while John vacillated between *we* and *you*. On the one hand, I knew John was the kind of guy who would appreciate a pregnancy being referred to as *ours*. On the other hand, until men started actually carrying and giving birth to babies, *we're pregnant* would probably continue to sound like hyperbole to my ears.

But bottom line, why even have the pronoun discussion when chances were that pregnancy wasn't going to happen to either of us?

"I guess I didn't really think so," I said, "but I spent a lot of time hearing about miracles during my formative years. You know, like Jesus feeding the masses from a couple loaves of bread. Or maybe it was Panera. I forget."

Somebody sighed. Maybe me, maybe both of us.

"Come on, don't get discouraged," John said. "We just started trying."

I didn't say anything.

"Do you think you should see somebody?" John said.

"You mean like for a tune-up and a lube job? Nah, you're supposed to try for six months before you start to panic. At least according to a quick Google search of

*what to expect when you're not expecting and you're
getting older by the minute.*"

"I've done a little bit of Googling, too. Maybe it
wouldn't be a bad idea to schedule an initial appointment with the best OB/GYN we can find, even ask her
to suggest a prenatal vitamin for you. I read that lots of
women start taking prenatal supplements early, just to
make sure they're in optimum shape when it happens."

"Sure," I said. "And maybe it wouldn't be a bad idea
for you to buy a few *Playboys* and practice shutting
yourself in a bathroom and producing sperm samples
on demand. Just to make sure you're quick on the draw
if it comes to that."

He didn't say anything.

"Listen," I said. "I can barely even allow myself to
think about this. I mean, what if we get our hopes up
and it doesn't happen?"

"Then we'll go to Plan B. But I think we've got to
give Plan A everything we've got first."

"We *are* giving it everything we've got. We've
ditched the condoms. I'm taking my basal temperature
and charting it so we know when I'm ovulating. We're
having sex at the right times, often enough but not so
often that it will deplete your sperm count."

I took a deep breath. "But I think it would really
help me out if we could be a little bit less intense about
the whole thing. You know, maybe we could pretend
we're just having lots of recreational sex because we
like it."

"Sure, not a problem. If it'll make it easier for you,
we can pretend to be rabbits. I'll bring the ears."

I smiled. "And the cottontails. Big fluffy ones."

After John and I hung up, I sat for a while, still holding my phone, staring into nothingness. Trying not to think, not to hope, not to set myself up for a fall. It had taken a lot for me to admit, even to myself, that I still wanted a baby. That John was onboard seemed like a small miracle, though my life being my life, not necessarily one that would lead to an actual child.

Oddly, moving in with John felt way scarier to me than having a baby with him. A baby is forever. Kids don't get bored and leave you for a better mother. With men, anything can happen.

I opened the single drawer of my bedside table. I took out the bottle of prenatal vitamins, unscrewed the top, fished one out.

I swallowed it down with a long swig from my water bottle.

Then I stared into nothingness some more.

. . . . .

By morning I'd decided that maybe a tune-up and a lube job wouldn't hurt after all. I was way overdue for a pap smear anyway.

I gulped down a cup of coffee and microwaved a breakfast sandwich.

I pulled up my address book on my phone. The Marshbury OB/GYN practice I usually went to was the same one my mother had gone to when she was alive, the one my sisters both went to, the one pretty much everybody I knew went to.

I pictured sitting down in the vast waiting room, running into someone my sister Carol had done an event for, or the mother of one of my students, or somebody I'd gone to high school with. Whoever it was would take one look at me and somehow just *know*. Maybe it was the way I sighed when she asked me how many kids I had just so she could show me pictures of hers. Or the pathetic way I rested one hand over my childless abdomen while I filled out my paperwork.

Before my pap smear had even gone off to the lab, my sister Carol would be on the phone to me. *So*, she'd say, *I hear you and John are trying to have a baby.*

I shook my head to dislodge the image. I sat down at my tiny kitchen table, fired up my laptop, did a quick search. Found a women's health center in a town about half an hour from Marshbury. It could be like a practice run. I'd just go in, get my pap smear, make sure my prenatal vitamins were up to snuff. Maybe I could even pick up a quick getting pregnant tip or two. I could say I was asking for a friend.

A woman's voice answered on the second ring. "Harbor Women's Health Center."

"Hi," I said. "I'd like to make an appointment."

"Is this an emergency?"

"No, no," I said. "No emergency. I just need the, you know, the usual."

"Have you been here before?"

"Nope," I said.

She gave me an after school appointment three days later. Given that it usually took me months to get a checkup appointment with my usual GYN practice, this seemed awfully quick to me. Maybe they'd had a can-cellation. Which just might mean my luck was changing.

I wiped the thought away so I didn't jinx myself. For extra measure I grabbed the saltshaker off the table and shook some salt over my left shoulder.

And then I knocked wood.

CHAPTER

Five

I gave my niece Siobhan another day to get back to me. When she didn't, I swung by my sister Carol's house on my way home from school.

I pulled my trusty old Honda Civic into the empty driveway. Carol and Dennis had four kids, which meant their garage was so jam-packed with everything from bikes, trikes and scooters to soccer and hockey equipment that I was pretty sure they hadn't been able to get a car in there for at least a decade.

I checked the time. Carol was probably chauffeuring Ian and Trevor to some kind of sports practice, but with luck Siobhan was home, either alone or babysitting Maeve. If not, I'd leave a note for her.

The back of my neck prickled as I cut across the lawn to the front door. I wondered if it was a sign that something was wrong, or simply that I'd read too much Nancy Drew as a child.

I gave a knock, pressed my ear to the door. Nothing.

I lifted the shell off a small verdigris turtle sitting on the front stoop near the welcome mat. My sister really needed to find a better place to hide her house key.

I knocked again, waited, opened the door.

"Yoo-hoo," I sang. "Anybody home?"

I found a pile of paper and a mug of markers in the playroom. Wrote CALL ME and my cell number in huge red letters.

Then I made my way to the kitchen. I took a quick break to open the fridge to see if there was anything inside that might necessitate inviting myself over for dinner. A bunch of chicken parts were marinating in something that didn't look all that intriguing.

I tried the freezer. An army of neatly stacked Tupperware containers saluted me. They were all labeled and dated. I tried to imagine becoming the kind of person who would spend an entire day cooking, dividing, labeling, freezing, just so my eating life could run smoothly for a week, maybe even two.

I shook my head, pulled out a rectangular container labeled MAC & CHEESE. I pried off the plastic lid, salivating as I took in the breadcrumbs that covered the top like a thick dusting of snow. I wondered for a moment if I could get away with taking it and leaving some money in its place. Decided it wasn't worth the aggravation of my sister freaking out.

I opened Carol's junk drawer, found a roll of tape, pulled off a long strip. Then I climbed the stairs to the second floor so I could tape the note to Siobhan's bedroom door.

My niece's door was closed. I felt that prickle again. Maybe I should do a little sleuthing around. Nothing really invasive. I could simply rifle through a drawer or two to see if any clues jumped out. Maybe I'd find a diary I could skim to help me figure out the best approach when Siobhan finally got in touch with me.

Siobhan was a great kid, and she and I had always been close. She'd crashed at my house a few times when she was fighting with her parents, a welcome break for both sides. She'd taught Irish step dancing back when I was running the afterschool program at Bayberry. She was lucky to have a hip, nonjudgmental aunt like me in her life.

A creak on the other side of the door made me jump.

"Siobhan?" I said.

Nothing.

I knocked lightly. Pressed my ear to the door again. The noise had stopped. Maybe I'd imagined it. Or maybe my niece was behind that door having sex with her boyfriend.

My heart beat wildly as my body went into fight or flight mode.

Flight was in the lead—I had a crazy urge to tape my note to the door and hightail it out of house. I'd make an anonymous call to my sister, disguise my voice, tell her to get home fast. Except that I'd have to figure out how to block my number so Carol wouldn't know it was me. Where oh where had all the payphones gone? I could understand cutting back on them now that practically everyone had a cellphone. But somebody should have thought to leave a few hanging around for family emergencies like this one.

I flashed on an image of my niece naked in bed, the faux stone of her bellybutton ring sparkling in the late afternoon sun coming through the window. Equally naked and entwined in a full body embrace with her was a big hairy testosterone-fueled teenage boy, who oddly looked exactly like the guy that had sat directly behind me in homeroom, breathing moist warm air on the back of my neck for all four years of high school. I stalled for a moment trying to remember the neck-breather's name. Ron? Don? Vaughn?

There are times when you just have to buck up and act like a grown up. I hated that. But I couldn't really see another option here.

I gave Siobhan's door a quick knock.

"Hi," I said in my perkiest voice as I turned the knob. "I'm so glad you're home!"

I pushed the door open. Then I jumped away from the doorway and pressed my back against the adjacent hallway wall, in case I'd accidentally interrupted a robber who was armed and dangerous. It was a move I'd picked up years before on *Charlie's Angels* and had yet to have an opportunity to use. Or maybe it was *Cagney and Lacey*.

I paused a discreet moment to give the big hairy boyfriend time to cover up. Or the robber time to jump out the window.

I counted *one Mississippi, two Mississippi* just to be sure.

I took a deep breath, pushed myself away from the wall.

"What's up?" my niece said when she saw me.

She was sitting on her bed, fully clothed in jeans and a Hello Kitty T-shirt, legs crossed at the ankles, the toes of her bare feet sparkling with turquoise polish. Leaning back against the headboard beside her was a fully clothed, tawny-haired, baby-faced boy who looked almost young enough that Siobhan could be babysitting him.

I took in their open laptops and matching headphones.

"What's going on?" I said, for lack of a better opening line.

Siobhan slid her earphones down until they circled her neck like a necklace. "Skype study group. Sorry, but I can't really talk right now because I have to get back to it. Oh, this is Jeremy. Jeremy, this is my Aunt Sarah."

"Hey," Jeremy said.

I ignored him and kept my eyes on my niece. "Can I speak to you privately for a moment?"

"But," she said.

"Now," I said.

Siobhan rolled her eyes, sighed, put her laptop and earphones on the bed beside her.

"We'll walk you to the door, Jeremy," I said.

He slid his earphones down. "Huh?"

"She's kicking you out," my niece said.

· · · · ·

"Of course you're having sex," I said. "I'm not that old."

Siobhan looked at me doubtfully.

"And I'm not an idiot," I said.

Siobhan's face didn't change.

"Sit," I said.

I grabbed us both water bottles from the fridge, sat down again at the kitchen table across from my niece. I opened mine and took a long sip while I tried to figure out where to go from here.

Siobhan looked at the water bottle I'd placed in front of her as if I might be trying to poison her.

"Say something," I finally said.

Siobhan leaned her elbows on the table, rested her chin on her fists. Then she crossed her arms over her chest and leaned back in her chair. "I'm not having sex."

"You've got the house to yourself and a boy in your bed. And how about that text you accidentally sent to me? *Babe? XO?* That sure doesn't sound like *I'm not having sex* to me."

"Fine. We make out sometimes, but that's it. Are you going to tell my mom?"

I blew out a puff of air. "You know I have to."

"Wait." Siobhan took her eyes off the water bottle long enough to give me a pleading look. "How about this, you don't tell my mom and I won't have Jeremy over any more unless my parents are home."

"I repeat," I said. "I'm not an idiot. How about this, I'll give you a chance to tell your mom before I do."

"Have you ever tried talking to my mom? She'll get all high drama and call his parents. She'll like totally ruin my life and make my dad back her up."

I took another sip of water as an idea came to me. I'd need to fine-tune some of the details, but it just might work.

"Listen," I said. "Let's both think about it tonight. I'll pick you up right after school tomorrow. You can take a ride with me and we'll talk about it some more."

"But—"

"Non-negotiable," I said.

CHAPTER

I had to admit that my niece had a pretty good handle on her mother's likely reaction. The ultimate goal was that Siobhan stay safe. Maybe she was sexually active. Maybe she wasn't. Maybe she wasn't now and she would be next month, or the month after that. But here's the thing: if two teenagers are bound and determined to have sex, there aren't enough adults in the world to stop them.

So my plan was that I'd take her with me to my appointment at the women's health center. Maybe Siobhan could take my appointment and I'd schedule a new one. Maybe once I explained the situation, they'd be nice enough to see us both. Especially if I pretended to be the mother and not the aunt. If Siobhan was too chicken to ask for a prescription for the pill, maybe I could ask for her, just so she had it when and if she needed it. And if all else failed, maybe we could swing by CVS and I'd buy her a case of condoms. Just in case.

Things got a little bit fuzzy after that. I'd tell my sister Carol after the fact, of course, but I'd present it in a way that made it sound spontaneous. Siobhan and I were taking a ride when I remembered I had an appointment, I'd say, and then one thing led to another. Carol might not thank me right away, but eventually she'd realize I'd done the right thing.

As soon as I got home, I called.

"Harbor Women's Health Center," a woman's voice said.

"Hi," I said. "My name is Sarah Hurlihy. I have an appointment tomorrow and I'd like to cancel it so that—"

"Are you safe?"

"Excuse me?" I said.

"Are. You. Safe."

I tried to wrap my head around her question. "As in safe sex, or safe to be around?"

"I'm going to remain silent," the women's voice said. "If you are *not safe*, please say *I agree*."

A long silence stretched between us.

I took a wild guess. "You're not an OB/GYN practice?"

"No, we're not. We're a women's health center and emergency shelter."

After we hung up, I sat for a while in my own little kitchen, wondering what kind of loser I was that I couldn't even successfully make an appointment for a pap smear. If I'd been trying for a passport, I probably would have ended up with a driver's license.

And who was I to think I could be of any help at all to my niece? She had a perfectly good mother for that. If Siobhan got mad at me for telling her mom what was going on, so be it.

And then there was John. I was pushing him away once more, turning him back into John Anderson again. Hiding my prenatal vitamins from him as if they were crack, not letting him in on something as basic as an initial pre-pregnancy trip to an OB/GYN. He would have loved to be included. And I had to admit that if he'd done the research, not only would I be sure I was taking the world's best prenatal vitamins right now, but I wouldn't have just had to cancel an accidental appointment at an emergency shelter.

The truth was that the only one I needed emergency protection from was myself. What was my *problem*? Why was I so bound and determined to screw up my life?

"Get your act together, Sarah," I said. "Before it's too late."

. . . . .

"That's hilarious," my sister Carol said when I finished telling her.

"It's not that funny," I said. "Plus the woman said it happens all the time. She was really good at her job though. If I *had* been in danger when I called, she's the one I'd want on the other side of the phone."

Carol crossed one ankle over the other. "When I was being released from the hospital after Maeve was born, the nurse told Dennis to leave the room. Then she asked me if I felt safe going home with an infant. I think the rest of it was, 'Do you fear for your safety or that of anyone else in the home?'"

"Wow," I said. I flashed on a quick image of me sitting in a hospital bed with an anonymous swaddled baby, but instead of John being asked to leave the room, the nurse told me to leave. *Do you think she can handle this?* she asked John once I was gone. *Do you fear for the baby's safety as well as your own?*

Carol sighed, snapping me out of my disaster fantasy. "I was tempted to tell her I needed to think about it for a few days just so I could catch up on my sleep, but I couldn't do it to Dennis. Anyway, I think that sort of thing is probably part of the intake assessment everywhere these days. It can be a tough, tough world out there."

Carol was sitting beside me on my couch. We'd taken off our sneakers. Our sock-covered feet were resting on my coffee table, and we were eating my famous Sarah's Winey Mac & Cheese. This was my go-to meal whenever I'd had a long day. Or didn't have any other food in the house. Or had just embarrassed myself by making an appointment at an emergency shelter for a pap smear.

Basically, you follow the directions on the Annie's Mac & Cheese box, with a few crucial changes. You cook the pasta, sprinkle on the cheese dust, skip the butter, substitute white wine for the milk. Then you serve it in wine glasses. Tonight I'd upgraded my specialty dish to borderline gourmet by putting in the butter after all (Kerrygold Irish) and sprinkling some bleu cheese (Black River) over the top of each serving.

Carol took another bite. "I hate to admit it, but this is ridiculously good."

"Thanks," I said. "I think."

"Okay, back to my darling daughter. I can't believe you didn't think I'd taken her to the gynecologist yet. She's seventeen."

"And I can't believe she already has a prescription for birth control pills."

"That doesn't mean she's taking them. They've been sitting unopened in her underwear drawer ever since—between her bras and her underpants."

"Not that you check or anything."

"Of course I check. At least once a week. And I count the condoms I put in her stocking, too."

"You put condoms in her *Christmas stocking*?" I shook my head. "I'm not sure that's good for Santa's image."

"I was discreet. I put them in a cute little drawstring bag along with some lip gloss."

I ran the spoon around the inside of my wineglass so I didn't miss any cheese. "Just promise me you won't tell Siobhan I told you. And it looked like they were just studying. Plus, *Jeremy* looks really young. He might not even have reached puberty yet."

"Oh, please." Carol put down her dinner wineglass and reached for her second wineglass, the one with wine in it. "It's those cute little androgynous boys you have to watch out for. Remember Herman from Herman's Hermits? Our babysitter used to have a mad crush on him?"

I launched into a rousing rendition of "I'm Henery the Eighth, I Am" and Carol joined in. My fake British accent was definitely better than hers.

"Ohmigod," I said. "Remember Mikey Higgins from high school? Long silky hair, about a hundred pounds soaking wet? All the girls were madly in love with him?"

"He had a massive crush on me," Carol said.

"Oh, please," I said. "You think everyone had a massive crush on you."

Carol sighed, slid over to the far end of my couch, swung her feet around so she could put them on the middle cushion. Her socks smelled like she needed new sneakers. "It's just that sometimes I wonder, you know? What would have happened if I hadn't gotten pregnant with Siobhan?"

"Stop." I put my own dinner wineglass down, slid over to the other side of the couch. "Don't you dare tell me the Saran Wrap story again."

Sadly it was already etched in my brain. Back when Carol and Dennis were dating in college, they couldn't find a condom once. So they used Saran Wrap. Just over nine months later Siobhan was born. Ever since my sister had overshared this detail, I hadn't been able to walk by a roll of Saran Wrap in the grocery store without imagining Dennis's penis wrapped in plastic. It was not a pretty sight.

"You guys are still happy, right?" The truth was that I'd never been all that crazy about Dennis. He was too corporate, too into golf and stupid jokes, too much a guys' guy for my taste.

"Yeah, we are. It's not that I wouldn't have wanted to end up with Dennis. It's just that sometimes I think of all the things I missed by getting married so young. Not so much other guys, although there's that, but other experiences—more travel, maybe some more school, definitely more time to sleep in on weekends. I used to tell myself that because I had my kids so young, once they were out of the house, I'd still be young enough to do it all. And then along came Maeve. By the time she graduates from high school, I'll be ancient."

"No worries," I said. "We'll all chip in and buy you a walker to celebrate."

"Funny. So funny I forgot to laugh. Anyway, my biggest fear is that it will happen to Siobhan. They say that the daughters of teen mothers who get pregnant out of wedlock are three times more likely to do the same thing themselves."

"*They* say a lot of things, but that doesn't mean it's going to happen. And besides, you weren't a teenager, and you and Dennis were barely out of wedlock, so it was just a technicality. Siobhan is a smart kid—there's no way she's going to mess up her life by getting pregnant."

I leaned over and grabbed my wine. Swung my feet up to claim the other side of the middle cushion, sniffed, wondered if maybe I was the one who needed new sneakers.

Carol reached for the wine bottle, topped off our glasses. "You have no idea what it's like now. You can practically put a high school pregnancy on your college applications under extracurricular activities. No shame, no blame. The kids just move into the basement with the baby and play house until they get bored, and then the grandparents are left holding the diaper bag."

"I'm so glad I teach preschool and not high school," I said.

"Well, I've got to tell you there's no way in hell I'm going directly from being the mother of a toddler to being a grandmother."

"Relax," I said. "We've got a plan. Just promise me you won't forget to act like I wasn't in on it, okay?"

"Cross my heart and hope to die."

"Stick a needle in your eye?" I said.

"Eww—that part seemed so much less disgusting when we were kids. But yeah. Especially since it might come in handy to have my darling daughter still like you once she hates my guts. That way you can still play good cop if we need you to."

We sipped our wine, each lost in our own thoughts.

"So," Carol said. "Why did you attempt to make a GYN appointment in another town anyway? Are you and John trying to have a baby?"

"Don't be ridiculous," I said. "Would I be drinking wine if I was trying to get pregnant?"

"Sure you would. If you'd just found out that you weren't."

CHAPTER

Seven

Polly and I were sitting in kiddie chairs at one of the low classroom tables. It was Friday and even the full-day kids had all either gone home or to childcare. We'd finished straightening up: The caps were back on the markers. All the stray pieces had been returned to the wooden puzzles. The assorted shoelaces and buckles and Velcro strips sewn on to the ends of each leg of our big stuffed lacing octopus had been untangled and were all set to go again on Monday.

Polly fished a Goldfish out of the Dixie cup she was holding and popped it into her mouth. I ran my hands under the edges of my child-size seat to make sure my thighs weren't starting to spill over too far. As a motivational fitness strategy, it wasn't half bad, kind of like a fat-measuring caliper that doubled as seating.

I'd taken down the calendar that hung on the inside of our supply cabinet door and placed it between us on the tabletop.

"Okay," I said. "Three good things that happened today and then we're out of here."

Polly thought for a moment. "Griffin didn't poop his pants once today."

"Woo-hoo," I said. *Griffin poop*, I wrote in tiny letters in red pen beneath today's date. Then I circled the word poop and drew a diagonal line through it.

"Kiley read *Llama Llama, Holiday Drama* to some of the three-year-olds. Or maybe she has it memorized—I couldn't really tell."

"It doesn't matter," I said. "Whether she's pre-reading or reading, she's on her way, which is so great."

I handed the pen to Polly. She wrote *Kiley read?* Then she added a series of exclamation points after the question mark.

I took the pen back and wrote *The reading nook is a huge hit.*

Polly beamed. She'd surprised me with the reading nook just after I'd hired her right before school started. It was made out of an entire small fiberglass boat tucked into the far corner of the room. Nautical-striped pillows cushioned the bottom. The stern was fitted out with a low bookshelf, a smaller bookshelf tucked into the bow. She'd stenciled READ READ READ YOUR BOOKS GENTLY THROUGH YOUR LIFE in big block letters on one side of the boat. The other side said MERRILY MERRILY MERRILY MERRILY READING IS A DREAM.

"Okay, that's three." I said.

I clicked the pen a few times, considered my new assistant. Her mostly brown hair, which had strands of silver running through it like tinsel, was pulled off her face and into a ponytail. She was wearing a slightly billowy teal top over simple black jeans and ballet flats, the perfect outfit for sitting on the floor with preschoolers. She looked better than she had when I first interviewed her. But her amber eyes were still underscored by dark circles, and her pale skin seemed even paler, making her freckles look as if they were about to jump off her face.

Polly was smart and she had a great attitude, but she had absolutely no previous classroom experience. She'd never even spent any time around children. After talking her into not having kids because he didn't think it was fair to the kids he'd already had with his first wife, her husband had left her for another woman. The breakup of her marriage had left her with a tendency to be accident-prone.

Even though my boss had preferred another candidate, I couldn't get Polly out of my mind. I'd been a total train wreck when my former husband left me. What if I'd decided to get out of Dodge the way Polly had, moved across the country, moved into a tiny winter rental on the beach where I didn't know a soul? And I needed a job, someone to take a chance on me.

So logic jumped out the window. I'd fought with my boss to hire Polly. And I'd won.

Polly and I were about the same age. Our stories were different in some ways, but in other ways they were pretty much the same story. Woman meets man and invests years of her life in him. Just as her childbearing years are winding down, man moves on to next woman. First woman says *WTF*. Eventually she figures out how to move on with her life.

The more time I spent with Polly, the more I liked her. In a parallel universe, I would have loved to hang out with her. But I'd learned the hard way how important it is for a teacher to maintain boundaries with her assistant, especially when a big part of your job is to boss that assistant around.

I'd also learned to be wary of those instant female friendships, the kind that burned too brightly, fueled by oversharing, and then disintegrated, leaving you exposed and vulnerable, your whole life story out there with someone you maybe didn't really trust after all.

I smiled. "So how's everything going?" I said, trying to strike the perfect balance between friendly and not-too-friendly.

There was a knock at the door. Ethan, whom I still thought of as EthanTheNewTeacher, stood in the doorway, a distressed leather backpack dangling from one shoulder.

"Hey," I said. "We were just talking about what a big hit our reading nook is. Thanks again for donating the boat to the cause."

He smiled, his perfect white teeth lighting up the room. "No problem. It was just sitting in my storage unit collecting barnacles."

Ethan's life had recently crashed and burned, too. He'd destroyed his marriage as well as a fledgling indie film career, totaled his car, wrecked his leg. When he bottomed out, our bitch of a boss was the only one who would take a chance on him. The good news was that Ethan loved teaching, and I could tell already that the kids were lucky to have him.

"Eleanor Rigby" started playing in my head like an auditory hallucination. The Beatles were right—there were so many lonely people in the world, more and more since John and Paul had written that song. I certainly knew what it felt like to be one of them. I pictured Polly and Ethan and all the others swimming in a sea of isolation as the slow minutes of an endless weekend ticked by. I was so incredibly lucky to have found John. Maybe once we were finally settled in to our new house, I'd invite Polly and Ethan both over, along with Lorna and Gloria and whoever else wanted to come, and we could all hang out together without crossing any boundaries.

"Well," Ethan said. He leaned one hand against the doorway, shifted his weight to his good leg. "I just wanted to say have a great weekend."

"Thanks." I started to push myself out of the chair while I still had the energy. "You, too."

He tilted his head at Polly. "I'll pick you up at seven, okay?"

. . . . .

By the time I made it out to my car, I'd come to terms with the fact that Polly and Ethan didn't need me to be their social director. I had to admit I didn't really need an assistant who was having a rebound relationship with the godson of our boss either. But it wasn't my business. And besides, it was Friday and I was officially off duty.

Out of the corner of my eye, I caught my ex's current wife Nikki attempting to herd their twins into a tank-like SUV. Kevin Jr. spun away from her, galloped across the parking lot, attempted to mount one of the boxwood duck topiaries that edged the walkway. Nikki Jr. took off in the opposite direction, stopped and yanked off one shoe, lobbed it into a thicket of forsythia.

"Ha," I said.

I put on my sunglasses. Then I got out of Dodge fast before my wasband's current wife had time to notice his starter wife.

I took my time getting to my sister's house, shaking off another school week and switching into weekend mode as I drove. When I pulled into the driveway behind Carol's minivan, Siobhan was sitting on her front steps, ear buds in, her face a perfect mixture of bored and pouting.

She walked slowly to my car, climbed in.

We rode wordlessly across town to Two Scoops, my favorite Marshbury ice cream store. I put the car into Park, took the key out of the ignition in case my niece was harboring escape fantasies, opened my door.

Siobhan just sat there.

"Single or double?" I said.

I watched her struggle: martyrdom vs. the fact that Two Scoops had amazing ice cream.

"Double," she said sadly. "Cookie Dough. No cone. Swedish Fish, Gummy Bears and Reese's Pieces."

I waited.

She sighed a long, ragged sigh. "*Please.*"

Siobhan was still in the car when I got back out, which seemed like a good sign. As I drove, I licked my single scoop Rocky Road with jimmies, or what non-New Englanders apparently called sprinkles, reaching chocolate sedation level as quickly as possible without giving myself an ice cream headache. We wound slowly up and down the roads in my favorite parts of town.

Siobhan sighed. I knew she wanted to ask me where we were going, but she didn't want to give me the satisfaction. I made a mental note of an OPEN HOUSE SATURDAY sign on a cute expanded Cape on a nice street that might or might not be in a flood zone.

Siobhan sighed again. I checked the time on my dashboard clock, looped around a few more neighborhoods. Marshbury property values tended to go up as you got closer to the beaches, but so did the property taxes. There were way too many stories in *The Marshbury Mirror*, the local weekly, about elderly couples whose mortgages had long been paid off being forced to sell their homes because they could no longer afford to pay the crazy high taxes as well as eat and buy heating oil.

Beside me, Siobhan sighed, crushed her empty ice cream dish in one hand, snapped her plastic spoon in half, sighed again.

I took a right and then a left, circled around the same block twice.

Carol's minivan was gone when I pulled into the driveway.

Siobhan stared straight ahead.

"So," I said. "I stayed up late last night thinking and thinking about this."

I paused to savor my last bite of sugar cone while I let the suspense build.

"Mmm," I said. "Delish. Okay, so if you can absolutely promise me, beyond a shadow of a doubt, that you will never, ever, under any circumstances, let Jeremy into your house when your parents aren't home—"

"Yeah, totally."

"Well . . ." I reached for a napkin, wiped my hands slowly, patted my mouth. "Then maybe I can let it slide this one time."

Her face lit up. "You mean you won't tell my mom?"

"Just this once," I said. "But I mean it, Siobhan. No boyfriend in the house unless your parents are home. I expect you to pinky swear and everything."

We locked pinkies on it.

CHAPTER

Eight

"Not to blow my own horn or anything," I said to Carol, "but I think I might have scared her straight."

"Maeve," Carol yelled. As soon as I'd dropped off Siobhan, I'd rendezvoused with Carol in the parking lot adjacent to Trevor's soccer practice. My niece Maeve had just decapitated her doll and thrown the head out the front window from her car seat, which was located in the backseat, grazing her mother's ear. The kid had an arm on her.

"Got it," I said. I jumped out of my car, grabbed the doll head, brushed it off. Took a moment to jog to the edge of the soccer field so my nephew Trevor would know I was here. I picked him out in the field, gave him a big wave. He lifted one hand a fraction of an inch, maybe a wave, maybe not.

I jogged back to the car and lobbed the doll head past Carol's head, barely missing her. Maeve grabbed it with both hands.

"Good reflexes," I said. "Where was I? Oh, Siobhan even pinky swore that she wouldn't let Jeremy into the house again unless you were home."

"Oh, please. Pinky swearing means nothing anymore."

"Sad," I said. "In our day, it always kept the boys out of the house."

My sister and I were quiet for a few moments, thinking about the boys we'd managed to sneak in and out when we were growing up. On the main floor of our house we'd had a back room that we used as a guestroom-slash-den-slash-playroom. With six kids and two adults living in there, there was no way anybody could get in and out of that window without somebody seeing it. The upstairs bedrooms weren't conducive to sneaking boys in and out either. Not only were there no strategically located trellises, but the house also had ten-foot downstairs ceilings and only a six-foot ladder in the garage.

It was possible to pry open the rusty old bulkhead door in the basement. But then you were stuck having a high school tryst in the cold, damp, fieldstone-walled, spider-infested basement.

The only place worth sneaking a boy into was what we all called the secret room. Unlike a Nancy Drew-esque secret room, where you might twist a knob or push a secret panel to get in, our secret room was accessed by opening the door from the kitchen to the mudroom.

Once you were standing in the little square postage stamp of a mudroom, if you opened the door straight ahead you'd enter a two-car garage that was old enough to have once housed horses and a buggy. But if you looked to your right and unlatched a tongue-and-groove wooden door instead, you could climb a rickety old staircase to an unfinished room over the garage.

Every surface of the room was covered in the same century-old knotty pine planks, darkened by time to a deep caramel. Walls turned into ceiling and met in a point overhead, providing a small central area where you could stand up straight. The only electricity came from an old brown extension cord running through a hole cut in the ceiling of the garage.

The secret room was artic cold in winter and hot as hell in summer. But on the days in between, it was the perfect place to drag our sleeping bags and pillows and pretend we were camping out. When we got older, Johnny grew anemic pot plants in front of the solitary window until he got caught and had to flush them down the toilet. Somebody else, or maybe all of us, stored contraband liquor there until eventually our parents found that, too, and took it away. *Just what the doctor ordered*, our father would say as he poured himself a drink with our booze in front of us.

Every single one of us, except maybe Billy Jr. who was a late bloomer, had managed to sneak a boyfriend or girlfriend into the secret room at one time or another. Christine even let a boyfriend who had temporarily run away from home live there for almost a week, and we all took turns hiding some of our dinner in a napkin, excusing ourselves to go to the bathroom, and sneaking up to feed him instead.

Our father had waxed on and on about adding a couple of dormers and turning the secret room into a rumpus room with a huge bar and swiveling barstools and maybe even a pool table. But our mother had always managed to veto his grand plans. Maybe she was afraid that once he disappeared up there, she'd never get him down again.

Carol looked at her watch, snapping me back to the present.

"Listen," she said. "I have to go. I've got to pick up Ian from lacrosse practice and get back here before Trevor is done with soccer. I'll call you as soon as I catch Siobhan in the act."

"Catch," Maeve yelled as she hurled the doll head out the car window again.

. . . . .

When I pulled into my driveway after meeting up with Carol, John and Horatio were playing Frisbee in my back yard. Even though John knew where I hid my spare key, he wasn't the kind of guy who'd use it unless he had to.

"How was the traffic?" I asked.

"Don't ask," he answered. Stellar weather was predicted for the weekend, which meant that everyone who'd been able to take off early from work must have been stuck in traffic along with John.

I let us all into the house and gave Horatio a bowl of water and a treat.

John ran back out to his car and returned with a bottle of wine and a big black and white polka-dotted gift bag shaped like a top hat.

I pulled the wine out of a brown paper bag. "Ooh, Educated Guess. What's the occasion?"

Educated Guess had become our special occasion wine. It was a Cabernet Sauvignon, rich and dark and multilayered, not that I was any kind of wine expert. Plus we both liked the name. As far as I was concerned, life was one big educated, and sometimes not so educated, guess.

"*We're* the occasion," John said. "Just you and me and a whole weekend ahead of us."

Horatio barked.

"Sorry, buddy, I didn't mean to leave you out." John squatted down and scratched Horatio's chest. Then he handed me the hat-shaped gift bag. I wrestled with the tissue paper and pulled out two sets of tall rabbit ears attached to headbands. The ears of one pair were lined in hot pink satin and the ears of the other pair in black satin.

"Very funny," I said. "As long as we don't actually have to wear them or anything."

He pulled me in for a kiss. "Of course we do. Tails are in the bag. I figured yours could double as a Halloween costume at school."

"Thanks. Although I'm not sure I could actually wear it without blushing."

So one thing pretty much led to another, and before we knew it we were in bed, naked as jailbirds and wearing his and her rabbit ears. We got so carried away we even forgot to bring the wine with us.

My doorbell rang, two loud notes managing to sound both insistent and annoying at the same time.

I rolled away from John, pushed myself up on my forearms. Debated whether or not I should bother to slip out of bed and peek out the window.

On the other side of my closed bedroom door, Horatio started barking like a maniac. His nails clicked and clacked on the hardwood floors of the hallway as he charged off to defend his pack from an intruder.

"It's probably UPS," I said. "Let's pretend we're not here. Unless you want to go sign for whatever it is. Just don't take the ears off. They're starting to grow on me."

He slid over in my direction. "No problem. I can sign Peter Cottontail."

I kissed him on the ticklish spot behind his rabbit ears. "Or Br'er Rabbit. Or—what were those rabbit movies Peter Sellers played Inspector Clouseau in?"

"*The Pink Panther*?"

"Oh, right," I said. "I always get rabbits and pink panthers mixed up. I have to tell you it does a number on my street cred as a preschool teacher."

Horatio went wild.

"Company," my father yelled from my doorway.

"Seriously?" I said.

. . . . .

By the time we'd ditched the rabbit ears, thrown on
jeans and T-shirts, and found him in the kitchen, my
father had already located my corkscrew and was
opening the Educated Guess.

"Be a good girl and fetch me a glass," he said by way
of greeting. "Anybody else care for a wee glass of fancy
pants wine to kick off the weekend?"

"How generous of you," I said as I kissed him on the
cheek. I opened a cabinet, pulled out three of the four
wine glasses I owned. Took a moment to remember
how pissed off I'd been when Kevin walked away with
our wedding present wineglasses, along with
everything else he felt like taking. *It's only stuff*, I'd
told myself at the time. But it had been my stuff, too.

How did people ever make themselves that
vulnerable to another person more than once in a
lifetime?

John waited until my father finished opening his
wine, then shook hands with him. Horatio barked some
more, hunkered down low over his front paws, raised
his hackles.

"Easy does it, sport," my father said to Horatio.
"This plan of ours will never work unless you behave
yourself."

John gave me his puzzled look. I shrugged.

Horatio barked some more.

"Where do you keep the whatchamacallits that make
him pipe down?" my father asked.

I pointed to the jar of dog treats on my kitchen counter.

My father unscrewed the lid, grabbed a treat, threw it up toward the ceiling.

Horatio caught it midair, swallowed it down in a single gulp. His hackles flattened out again and his tail started wagging like crazy. Though my father had never been much of a dog fan, I had to admit he was certainly good at manipulation.

"Now we're cooking with gas," my dad said. "Just remember, young fella, if you play your cards right, there's lots more where that came from."

My father poured three glasses of Educated Guess, grabbed the fullest one. He raised his glass in the direction of my kitchen table. "Sit."

Horatio sat.

John and I looked at each other. I shrugged again.

We joined my dad at the table.

He held up his glass. "*Being Irish, he had an abiding sense of tragedy, which sustained him through temporary periods of joy.*"

"Yeats?" I said, partly to show off and partly to try to keep it from turning into a full-length recitation.

"Good girl. The apple doesn't fall far from the pie, as I've been wont to say."

"*Education is not the filling of a pail, but the lighting of a fire,*" I said, adding my Yeats to my father's.

"Sláinte!" my father roared. We clanked glasses all around.

My dad took a sip of John's and my special wine, scrunched his eyes shut while he rolled it around in his mouth, gave it a thumbs up.

"You know," he said, "you were quoting the masters when you were knee high to a grasshopper, Christine."

"Sarah," I said.

My father slapped his knee. "Just making sure you're awake, Sarry girl. Okay, here's the rub. I need to borrow the dog."

"Dad," I said. "John's dog isn't a cup of sugar. You can't just borrow him."

CHAPTER

Nine

John and I were on the way to our first Saturday afternoon open house of the day.

"Take a left at the next corner," I said. "Are you absolutely positive you're okay with Horatio hanging out with my father for a few hours?"

"I wouldn't go quite that far, but I think I'm fairly certain." He put on his left blinker. "Although I have to admit I'd feel slightly more confident if he'd remember to call him Horatio instead of Homer."

"That's my dad," I said. "And just in case you think he's referring to the guy who wrote the *Iliad* and the *Odyssey*, my guess is the name change might just as easily have been inspired by Homer Simpson."

"D'oh!" John said as he hit his forehead with the heel of one hand. His Homer Simpson imitation wasn't funny enough to make me laugh, though this late in the trajectory of Homer Simpson imitations it was doubtful that anybody else's could either, but it made me smile. It's easy to get a quick laugh out of somebody, but in a way it's more impressive to keep them smiling. John had that earnest, endearing, smile-inspiring something.

"The way I'm looking at it," John said, "this lets us check out your dad's dog-sitting proficiency without committing to anything. I've been trying to get a picture of how things will play out once I move down here. I mean, Horatio will be all set if I'm working remote, but when I have to drive in for meetings, it's a long haul for him just to spend a few hours at puppy playcare. Plus, I'd have a tough time dragging him back out of there since he's used to a longer stint."

"Well," I said. "It would be pretty amazing if my father actually came in handy for a change. But it still doesn't quite add up. Why would he try to get a job as a dog walker? My father and dogs don't exactly fit together like preschoolers and Playdoh. Take a right at the next light."

John slowed to a stop even though the light was barely yellow, instead of barreling through it the way Kevin would have when we were still married, just to prove he could.

"I thought your dad explained it pretty well while he drank my wine," John said.

"Sorry about that. I'll replace it."

"No need. But we might want to consider investing in a few decoy bottles for the future."

"Genius," I said. "Two Buck Chuck from Trader Joe's—I'm on it."

"I think it's admirable that your dad doesn't want to turn into an old fuddy duddy, to use his words, sitting around reading the obituaries all day long. What did he call them again?"

"The Irish sports page," I said. "Which might explain where I inherited my cheery world view, in case you've been wondering."

"Thanks for pointing that out, Sunshine." The light changed and John made the turn. "He's right though. Retirement was invented when the average life expectancy was about eighteen months after retirement. Life is getting longer. Your dad could live to be a hundred."

"I wouldn't put it past him."

"Getting a job as a dog walker will get him out in the fresh air, bring in some extra money. It's a great idea."

I shook my head. "All I know is that there has to be at least one woman involved."

. . . . .

"It can only go up from here," John said. We were standing in front of an open house sign and gazing at a rickety beach bungalow with three tiny mismatched additions.

"Wanna bet?" I scrolled through the listing on my phone. "I can't believe they had the audacity to call this place *expansive*."

John was looking over my shoulder. "We should know by now not to fall for *just needs a little TLC*. But the flip side is that at this price point we could consider a major renovation."

"I don't know," I said. "It's definitely an old summer house, and it probably hasn't even been winterized. And it has to be in the flood zone, so we'd have to factor in the cost of flood insurance. Maybe we should just skip it and move on to the next one."

John looked down at the virgin page on his clipboard. "We're here, so I say we take a quick peek. If nothing else, it'll make us appreciate the next house we see."

The house was exactly what I'd thought it would be. Knotty pine paneling. Orange shag carpeting reeking of mildew. Smoke-yellowed dropped ceiling panels held in place by a crosshatch of beige metal frames. A bathroom that you entered through a door next to the refrigerator and across from the stove.

I sneezed.

"Bless you," the realtor said. "So what do you think?"

"Thank you," I said. "I think it looks like a ton of work."

"Not really. It's practically all cosmetic." The realtor waved one gold ring-studded hand to show what a piece of cake it would be. She had expensive blond hair, and her makeup had been applied to her face so thickly that her neck seemed to belong to another person.

John backed his way out of the bathroom to join us in the kitchen. "The house is in a great location, but I think it's a total teardown."

The realtor opened her mouth, closed it again.

"Well," I said. "Thanks so much. Have a nice open house."

"Are you working with anyone yet?" the realtor said. "I have some other properties I can show you."

"Thanks," John said. "But we're all set."

Our plan was to stick with cruising the house listings on the Internet and going to open houses. If we found a house we loved, we'd take it from there. But we didn't want to choose a realtor to work with until we had to. I wasn't sure about John, but the failure of my marriage had left me with a kind of general commitment phobia that included everything from realtors to cellphones. Even though I'd been due for a free cellphone upgrade ages ago, I found myself hanging onto my old phone because I didn't want to sign another two-year contract. Two years was a long time. Anything could happen.

"Let's try the expanded Cape next," I said. "Maybe we'll get lucky."

I gave John directions to the house I'd discovered while driving around with Siobhan. It had teal trim and white cedar shingles that had weathered to a silvery grey, plus a decent-sized fenced-in backyard that Horatio would love. Three cars filled the driveway, so we pulled in behind another car parked along the side of the road.

John opened the door and let me walk through first. A staircase stopped me almost immediately. We walked through the small boxy rooms, excusing ourselves as we navigated past another couple.

"Hi, I'm Claustrophobic," I whispered to John. "What's your name?"

"Maybe we could take down some walls," he whispered back. "You know, open it up a little."

We climbed the stairs, stopping midway to press our backs against the wall so a couple that looked barely old enough to date, let alone buy a house, could get by us.

The upstairs bathroom seriously needed to be brought up to this millennium. The first two bedrooms were just okay, with small closets and the kind of sharp ceiling angles that look charming in magazine pictures, but make you bump your head in real life.

We stepped out into the hallway again to let a couple coming up behind us take their turn viewing the room. Another couple stepped into the third bedroom. "Ooh," we heard the woman say.

We followed them in.

It was the perfect baby's room. Sage walls, lavender accents, white crown molding. A simple but elegant white crib floated in the center of the room on a lavender and sage-striped rug. Soft late afternoon sunlight streamed in through a paned window above a built-in window seat. A rocking chair holding a great big stuffed teddy bear with a sage and lavender bandanna around its neck was tucked into one corner. The small white bookcase adjacent to the chair was bursting with picture books. A hand-lettered sign perched on top of the bookcase read *Once Upon a Time.*

The other couple, probably a good decade younger than John and me, was gazing reverently at the crib, taking in the sage and lavender plaid bumper tied to the crib rails, the mobile of a cow jumping over the moon hanging above the crib. The woman rested one hand on her very pregnant belly. Seven months? Eight? The man reached a hand over, and they both stroked her beach ball-shaped stomach.

John was mesmerized.

"Come on," I whispered. "Let's get out of here."

We walked single file down the narrow carpeted stairs.

"Can I ask you to sign in, please?" a realtor's chirpy voice said.

It was Nikki.

CHAPTER

Ten

I froze, four or five steps from the bottom, my head cut off from view by the low overhead, John right behind me. My wasband's wife hadn't seen me yet. If we could simply back our way up a few steps, then turn around and act like we wanted to take another peek, we could hide out on the second floor until she was busy with another couple in the kitchen, or even in the backyard. And then we could make a run for it.

"Sarah?" John said.

Nikki leaned sideways so she could see up the stairs. "Sarah!"

"Hi," I said. "We were just leaving."

On that cue, John started moving again. When I didn't, he bumped into me. I slid down the final stairs, the soles of my flats skimming the edges of the carpeted steps. John grabbed my shoulders. I sat down hard on the bottom step. He kept going, jumping over me as if we were playing leapfrog. Or stuck in a bad rerun of *I Love Lucy*. His clipboard landed in my lap.

"Oh, Ricky," I said, for lack of a better line.

John actually got it. "Hi, honey, I'm home," he said as he reached out a hand to help me up. "Are you okay?"

I handed him his clipboard. "Mentally or physically?"

"Oh, you two are too cute," Nikki said.

"Thanks," I said. I pulled my sweater down until it covered the waistband of my jeans again. "Um, this is John. John, Nikki."

Nikki held out her hand. "I'm Kevin's wife. You know, *that* Kevin. You've probably heard all sorts of things about me, but I just want you to know that hardly any of them are true." She laughed like this was funny.

John gave her hand a quick shake. "Kevin who?" he said.

In that moment, I'd never loved him more. He reached an arm around my shoulders.

Her face fell. "Oh, I'm so sorry." She looked at me, dropped her voice to a whisper. "Does he not know you've been *married*?"

"I only told him about the first five times," I whispered back.

John laughed. "Nice to meet you, Nikki."

"You, too." She opened her eyes wide. "So you're buying a house together!"

John and I each took a perfectly synchronized step in the direction of the door.

"Would you mind signing in first?" she said. "The more people show up, the better I look. Here, it's right this way."

John and I looked at each other, then followed her into the kitchen. When choosing a replacement wife, I had to admit it looked like my ex-husband had gone shopping and picked out the first woman he found that looked a little bit like me but younger. Wife One and Wife Two were about the same height and build, medium-length brown hair, dark eyes, big smiles, not that I'd done much smiling when I was with Kevin, especially in the last few years. I knew better than to take Nikki's and my resemblance as any kind of compliment—it was more about my former husband's lack of vision.

I grabbed the pen next to the sign-up sheet, signed my name and wrote my real address, since after all it had once been Kevin's address, too. Then I transposed two letters on my phone number and left the email field blank.

"The twins just love it at Bayberry," Nikki was saying. "Nikki Jr. is tying her shoes already, and Kevin Jr. actually took his own backpack out of the car and carried it all the way into the house by himself."

"Terrific," I said. "Well . . ."

Nikki handed John one of her business cards. "Are you working with anyone yet? I've got a couple of great listings I can show you." She lowered her voice to a whisper again. "Much better than *this* place."

She looked at me, then at John, then at me again. "And if you want me to take a look at your house and give you a price estimate, I can do that, too. Kevin and I have driven by a few times, but I'd really have to get a good look at the inside to be accurate."

"Thanks," John said. "But we're all set with a realtor."

"Okay," Nikki said. "Then why don't you two come over for dinner tonight? Big Kevin would love it and so would the twins."

"Thanks," I said. "But we're all set with dinner, too."

. . . . .

"Ohmigod," I said once we were safely back in John's car. "Just give me a century or two to recover from that."

John laughed. "It wasn't *that* bad. But just out of curiosity, exactly how big is Big Kevin?"

"Not that big. But I could start calling you Big John once in a while if it would make you feel better. Especially if you're wearing your rabbit ears."

"Thank you. I'd appreciate that."

"And I am not going to ask you who's prettier," I said. "Because that would make me shallow and insecure."

"Of course you're prettier. Hands down."

"Thanks. How nice of you to say that without any pressure from me." The good news was that running into Nikki had almost erased the memory of the perfect baby's room John and I might never have. I shook my head. "Call me crazy, but maybe we should seriously consider looking for a house outside of Marshbury."

John put the keys in the ignition, turned to look at me. "Why? Didn't you say your ex doesn't even live in town? And it's not like he and Nikki can't put our new house on their drive-by list as long as we're within a tank of gas. Or two."

"Thank you so much for that lovely image." I reached for my seatbelt. "Okay, then maybe we should think about buying a house in Poland. I hear it's beautiful this time of year. Whatever time of year it is in Poland. And not to sound paranoid or anything, but let's get out of here fast before you-know-who comes running out to ask us if we want to meet up after dinner for a movie."

John started his car, executed a perfect three-point turn. "We've been through all this. There's an upside and a downside to everything, and I thought we'd finally agreed that the upside to living in Marshbury beats the downside."

I pulled up the address of the next open house on my phone. "Take a left at the end of the street. Yeah, I know. It's just that I'm also starting to worry that we'll never find a house here. Most of the ones we've seen aren't any better than *my* stupid house. Even the ones that are crazy expensive still need work. And I don't want us to be house poor. I've already been there, done that."

At some point during the extended blur surrounding the death of my mother and my husband moving out on me, it was decided that I would keep my house. Neither Kevin nor my father thought to discuss this with me. My father showed up one day a couple of months after Kevin left, which was a couple of months after my mother died, and handed me a bank check. I wondered if the money came from my mother's life insurance. I didn't ask.

"What's that?" I'd asked, looking at the check from a safe distance.

"It's good riddance to bad rubbish." My father had always said to anyone who would listen that Kevin wasn't on his best day good enough for me.

"Dad, I don't want your money."

"One day soon it will all be yours anyway. Don't make me die first to take care of my little girl. Take it, Sarry, with my blessing." My father had smiled bravely, as if one foot had already gone over to the other side. He'd always had an amazing ability to add or subtract decades to his life as it suited him. At this moment he'd looked and sounded more like my grandfather than my father.

"No, really," I'd said. I didn't even like the house that much. Kevin and I had bought the three-bedroom, one-bath, '50s-style ranch as a starter home, planning to fix it up and move on to something better. And then Kevin had moved on to Nikki.

I'd taken the check, bought out Kevin's half of the house, supplemented my teaching income by running Bayberry's afterschool program for a while, working at Bayberry summer camp, even doing a summer consulting gig at the company John worked for. Every month I squeaked by.

The exact amount of the check my father had given me was still seared on my brain. The second I sold my house, I'd pay him back every cent.

"I don't want us to be house poor either," John said. "Between the sale of your house and the rental income from my condo, we're going to be all set. All we have to do is find the right house."

"Go straight at the lights. Well, that brings me back to my stupid house. I can't believe some of the ones we've seen are even more pathetic, not less."

John stopped at another yellow light. "Well, if push comes to shove, we could always think about transforming your place. You know, bring in an architect, maybe add a second floor, or give it more of a contemporary feel by going out instead of up with additions at either end—picture a U-shape going out to the back with a courtyard in the center of it. Big master bedroom—"

"No way," I said. "The two of us living in the house where my marriage failed would entirely jinx any chance we have for happiness."

"Not if we completely reinvented it. And if making it unrecognizable isn't enough, we could consider having an exorcism. Or burning some sage."

"There's not enough sage in the world," I said. "Okay, it's the next driveway on the right. Great, wouldn't you know it's the ugly house."

We pulled into the driveway and looked past the OPEN HOUSE sign. The second floor of the house hung over the first floor like a set of buckteeth, and the one tiny window on the right side of the second floor didn't line up with the two big mismatched windows on the left side. I pulled up the listing photo on my phone and tried to reconcile it with the house we were looking at.

"Even I say we skip this one." John reached over and put his hand on my thigh. "Let's call it a day and go pick up Horatio and take a walk on the beach instead."

CHAPTER

Eleven

Three strange cars shared the blue-and-white crushed mussel shell driveway with my father's sea green Mini Cooper. Actually, one of the vehicles was an ice cream truck. Another was a Granny Smith green Volkswagen convertible bug with the top down and an oversize silk daisy decorating the antenna. The third car, a bumblebee-yellow jeep with a bumper sticker that read SEXY SALSA DANCER INSIDE, looked almost like a wallflower by comparison.

"I didn't know ice cream trucks came in pink," John said.

"And to think I was worried about my father getting over Sweepstakes Sally," I said. Sweepstakes Sally had been my father's last bad girlfriend in a long string of them. He'd fallen hard for her, become temporarily addicted to online sweepstaking, accidentally proposed to her, only to eventually realize she was scamming him. The good news was that his computer skills had improved dramatically, and he'd also been pretty generous about sharing his sweepstakes spoils, including sidewalk chalk for my classroom and a case of disposable wipes, which are a teacher's best friend.

My phone rang. I pulled it out of my purse, thinking it might be my dad asking John and me to drive around the block a few times before we crashed his party. On the one hand, this is not something you ever want to be asked to do by your father, but on the other hand, you don't necessarily want to walk in on his shenanigans either.

It was Carol. "I'd better take this," I said, "or she'll just keep calling. Do you want me to meet you inside?"

John opened his Heath Bar eyes wide. "Are you kidding me? There's no way in hell I'm going in there without you. I just hope your father hasn't forgotten about Horatio."

"Okay, I'll make it quick." I pushed the Yes button on my cell. "Hey, what's up?"

"My eldest daughter has been officially caught in the act."

"Already? Wow, that was fast. How did you do it?"

"I told her we were all taking a family day trip out to Western Mass to go apple picking, then made her work really hard to wiggle out of it because of a term paper she supposedly had to write. Dennis and I took the younger kids out for breakfast, swung by Stop 'n' Shop to pick up a bag of apples. Then Dennis dropped me off at the corner and brought the kids and the apples to the playground."

"Diabolical."

"Yeah, well, I do my best. So I skulked down our street, snuck in through the back door, and the rest is history."

"Were they in her bedroom?" I asked.

"Nope, watching a movie on the couch in the living room. Fully clothed, but blankets and pillows were involved, so it was only a matter of time. Minutes or months, it doesn't really matter. I read them both the riot act, threatened to call Jeremy's parents if he ever set foot in the house again when we weren't home. And Siobhan is officially grounded for life, with the slim possibility of parole after the first of the year. She's no longer allowed to use Dennis's and my cars or stay home alone, which means she'll be driving around with me and doing her homework in the back of my minivan, unless she's legitimately involved in an after school activity. And. I. Will. Check."

"Wow," I said. "She'll be joining every extracurricular activity she can find."

"Great. She could use a few more, or we'll never get her out of the house and off to college. That was the whole point of her not working part time at the movie theater this year."

I held up one finger to tell John we were almost finished. "Okay, so what do you need from me?"

"Nothing right now, but I'll keep you posted. How's it going with the house hunt?"

"Don't ask. Listen, I have to go. I'll talk to you later." I hung up fast before she could start meddling.

I gave John the Cliff Notes version.

"Wow," he said. "She seems like such a great kid."

"She is," I said. "It's just what teenagers do. Developmentally her job is to try to get away with things like this, and her family's job is to catch her."

John nodded as if he were filing this away for future reference. "Do you know that before I met you, I thought Siobhan was pronounced SEE-oh-bahn instead of Sheh-VOHN."

I rolled my eyes. "You are soooo not Irish. Come on, let's get in there and rescue Homer."

We wound our way through the cars in the driveway, slowing down to take in three identical turquoise-and-white signs on the sides of each vehicle that read BARK & ROLL FOREVER.

"Aha," I said in my best Nancy Drew imitation. Or maybe it was Columbo. "The pieces are starting to come together."

. . . . .

My father was stretched back on his worn vinyl recliner, in full entertainment mode. "Well, at first I supposed that the 72-inch flat screen would go right there over the fireplace, but after further deliberation I concluded that I might want to keep it a bit more hidden for atmospheric purposes. So the new and improved plan is to build myself a man cavern."

"Man cave," I said.

"That, too," my father said.

Horatio gave us a quick yip and a tale wag. Then he sighed and went back to getting his ears scratched by one of the three women who were sitting on the couch I'd grown up with. They were all wearing hot pink BARK & ROLL FOREVER T-shirts and black spandex capri tights with hot pink racing stripes. Their white Skechers sneakers were the kind that had memory foam insoles.

"Grab yourselves a couple of chairs and take a load off," my father said. "I was just telling these lovely ladies about the Renovate Your Dad sweepstakes you kids almost won for me."

"Hi," I said. "I'm Sarah and this is John."

"He belongs to Homer," my father said. "All blarney and taradiddle aside, I'm fairly sure I can reel him in as a client."

"Homer's a great dog," the women scratching Horatio's ears said. "Billy was just telling us he's half Chihuahua and half tall, handsome blind date?"

The other two women laughed.

"Close," John said. "Actually he's half Yorkie and half greyhound. And by the way, his name is Horatio."

"Nothing wrong with a good mutt," my father said. "We're all mixed breeds at this point in the passage of time. Even the Irish, though I have to say our genes hold up better than most."

A moment of silence followed as the rest of us tried to figure out what my father's statement might possibly mean.

"Oh," one of the other women said. "I'm Betty Ann and this is Doris and Marilyn."

"Nice to meet you," John and I both said.

"Can Sarah get anybody anything?" my father asked, as if I were a waitress and they were sitting in my station.

"No thanks," the third woman said. "We're all set." She leaned forward and pulled a small plastic water bottle out of one of the holster-like loops on the belt she was wearing. She pulled the top into open position with her teeth and took a long swig. The other two women were wearing the same belts, each with four small bottles of water evenly distributed around their waists.

"I think I'll stick to tea instead of giggle water, honey," my father said. "Given that we're in the midst of an interview and all."

"Sorry to interrupt," John said. He started to push himself out of his chair. "We'll just grab Horatio—"

"Not at all," Betty Ann, who appeared to be the ringleader, said. "We were just wrapping things up. Bark & Roll Forever has been all female up until now, but the girls and I think Billy will shake things up a bit."

"He's certainly good at that," I said.

"Great name for a business," John said.

"Thanks," Betty Ann said. "It had the boomer vibe we were going for. Plus it's the thing I love most about dogs. They know how to live. They'd be happy to just bark and roll forever."

"Woof," my father said.

All three women cracked up. "Oh, Billy," one of them said.

"So how does it work?" John said. "Are you exclusively a dog-walking service, or do you also have a facility for daycare and boarding?"

"All of the above," Betty Ann said. "It keeps us hopping, even with a handful of interns from the local high school helping us out. Which leaves us precious little time for marketing. So the plan is for Billy to drive around in the ice cream truck, stopping wherever the dogs are and handing out treats and business cards."

"Does that mean I've got the job?" my father said.

The three women looked at one another.

"We'll get out of your way and let you wrap things up in private," I said before I got stuck actually having to wait on anybody.

John and I stood. Horatio jumped down from the sofa.

"Better take him out the kitchen door," my father said. "Homer makes a wild ruckus when he gets anywhere near that front porch."

Twelve

Dear Bayberry Parents,

Halloween will soon be upon us. This is one of our students' favorite holidays, and rest assured that your child's teachers will take full advantage of the many wonderful opportunities it provides for age-appropriate learning and celebration.

Please do your part by adhering to the following ironclad, nonnegotiable rules:

While parents are cordially invited to attend the Bayberry Halloween Costume Parade (separate invitation to follow), remember that parents will be in attendance solely to cheer on their offspring and not to be their hand servants. Students' costumes should be manageable enough to be under the full control of the student for an entire school day. Additionally, all masks, as well as all accessories and embellishments that hinder timely bathroom access on the part of the child, are strictly prohibited.

Bayberry Preschool does not facilitate Halloween costume competition or awards of any kind. Costumes are expressly for the enjoyment of the children. Please allow your child to be a part of the decision-making as well as the costume-creating process—think home-made vs. store-bought, simple vs. elaborate. And please do refrain from hiring professional costume designers.

Ponies and other livestock, as well as pets, are prohibited from the Bayberry Halloween celebration, regardless of their thematic relationship to your child's costume. Instead, please substitute toy versions of these animals measuring less than 12" (twelve inches) in all directions.

Weapons, real or toy, including guns, squirt guns, cap guns, swords, bayonets, hand grenades, and knives, are strictly prohibited as well. Also strictly prohibited are motorized vehicles as well as remote-control planes, helicopters, and yes, drones.

Costumes that are edible in whole or in part are also prohibited. And please remember: Do not send candy in your child's lunch, on Halloween or on any day. Our experience is that Bayberry parents are better able to deal with the repercussions of their offspring's sugar highs in the safety of their own home.

Warmly,
Kate Stone, Principal

"Well," Polly said as put the letter back on the pile. "She certainly covered all the bases."

"Ha," I said. "Just wait. We'll send the letters home in the kids' backpacks tomorrow, which means my phone will be ringing off the hook tomorrow night with parents wanting to know does it really mean that their child can't drive her Barbie jeep in the Halloween parade, because she's got her heart set on being Malibu Barbie and everybody knows that nobody in California walks anywhere."

"Better you than me." Polly fished a Goldfish out of her Dixie cup and popped it into her mouth.

"Yeah, not having to field phone calls is definitely one of the perks of being the assistant and not the lead teacher." I took a sip from my water bottle. "A few years ago we had a three-year-old who showed up dressed like a chocolate chip cookie, with big hunks of real chocolate glue-gunned all over him. Just before snack time, a couple of the kids started yanking them off and eating them, and before we knew it we had a preschool mob scene—they practically mauled the poor kid before we got to him."

"The smell of chocolate does that to me sometimes, too," Polly said.

"And then there was the five-year-old who came in dressed as a Christmas tree with a big plastic bubble over her head. She was supposed to be a snow globe, but her parents seriously underestimated the appropriate size for the air holes. We found her keeled

over in the corner of the room with her trunk sticking
up in the air."

"Whoa," Polly said. "Was she okay?"

"Yeah, we just yanked off her globe and kept her
outside in the fresh air until the school nurse showed
up and gave her the all-clear. But one of my all time
favorites was this four-year-old who decided he wanted
to be a Slinky dog. He envisioned his entire ensemble
right down to the last detail. His mom and dad took
him shopping and eventually they found the mustard-
colored sweat suit he was looking for. Then they
bought rectangles of matching felt so they could help
him cut out ears and sew them onto a knitted cap.
Their final stop was the hardware store, where he
picked out the exact gauge wire he wanted. And on the
big day, he instructed them to wrap it around and
around and around his body until his Slinky dog vision
came to life."

"So creative," Polly said. "And how great that his
parents supported him like that."

I nodded. "He even figured out how to go to the
bathroom by peeing between the coils. Getting his
sweatpants back up was a bit more complicated though.
And he had to spend the whole day standing. But I
think he felt good about suffering for his art."

Polly reached for another Goldfish. "Do you know
what happened to him? I mean, is he now a costume
designer on Broadway, or the creative director of a
famous advertising agency?"

I shrugged. "I think he's probably rocking his way
through fourth or fifth grade right about now."

"Do you ever stay in touch with the kids? You know, once they graduate?"

"Sometimes, especially if they have younger siblings. But I think it's usually the teachers they have when they're a little bit older that they tend to remember."

"Ohmigod," Polly said. "Mrs. Forest. She was my kindergarten teacher, and I was bound and determined to marry her. In hindsight, she might have been a better choice than the guy I did marry."

"Sister Cecelia Bernadette," I said. "Fourth grade. I had older siblings, and our mom spent lots of time working with us, so I was way ahead of some of the other students. She put me to work tutoring the kids who needed it. I don't think I'd ever felt that special. I remember floating around her classroom like I was walking on air."

"Do you think that's why you became a teacher?"

"Maybe," I said. "Though I also remember desperately wanting to be a nun for a few years. Until I got my hands on my older sister's stash of *Tiger Beat* magazines and discovered boy bands."

I slid a piece of cardboard across the table to Polly. "Okay, let's get to work or we'll never get out of here. How are you at drawing bats?"

Polly grabbed a pencil and tapped the eraser side on the table a few times. "How big?"

"About the width of a preschooler's hand, and maybe half that for the height."

In fewer than a dozen strokes of her pencil, Polly nailed it: the span of the bat wings, the points of the ears and the body, the way the lower part of each wing had a series of rolling dips like upside-down ocean waves.

"Wow," I said. "I would give anything to be able to draw like that. Or even to be able to take credit for hiring you because you could draw. I can't believe I never even thought to ask."

Polly shrugged. "It's really just training your eyes to see. I haven't done much of it for years, but drawing gave me a place to disappear to when I was a kid, a whole imaginary world where I was never alone."

"Alone?" I said. "What's that?"

Polly shook her head. "Alone was the theme of my childhood. Only child, no pets, much older parents that weren't quite sure what to do with me once they finally had me."

I closed my eyes against the image of John's and my imaginary child one day describing us this way. Then I tried to picture us having more than one child, but it seemed like too much to hope for. At least John had Horatio, who qualified as a pet, and I could certainly bring plenty of cousins to the mix to help ward off the aloneness.

I handed Polly one of our two pairs of teacher scissors. "Are your parents still alive?"

She looked up from cutting out her bat. "No. They both died when I was in my twenties. In hindsight, I think I probably jumped into my marriage so I wouldn't feel quite so untethered. In the end, it turned out to be just a different kind of alone."

I grabbed the other pair of scissors and began cutting short strips of inch-wide elastic. "Pretty much the only time I was ever alone when I was a kid was in the bathroom, and not for long because somebody was always banging on the door. But I found this hideaway on the shady side of our house—I had to crawl under all these overgrown rhododendrons to get there. On hot summer afternoons I used to stay out there for hours doing handstands against the side of the house. You can probably still see the scuffmarks from my heels on the shingles."

Polly handed me her bat. I finished cutting the elastic strips, and then I traced the bat template over and over again on a big sheet of black poster board. When I'd filled every available space with bat shapes, I slid the poster board over to Polly so she could start cutting them out while I traced more bats on a second sheet of poster board. When we had enough bats for all the kids and Polly and me, plus five extras for backup, I jumped in on the cutting.

Once we had our bevy of bats, I spread a piece of elastic horizontally across one, made sure it was centered, stapled it at either end. I slid my index finger through the elastic and waggled the bat at Polly.

She grabbed another piece of elastic, made her own.

We wiggled our bat finger puppets at each other, grinning like kids.

"So that's what the teachers do when the kids go home!" someone yelled from our doorway.

We turned toward an annoying giggle. Nikki.

Nikki Jr. and Kevin Jr. made a mad dash for our bats. Their mother just stood there.

Polly started scooping up the bats while I pushed myself free of my chair and got down low. I looped an arm around each Junior, herded them through the doorway, pulled the door closed behind me.

"Nice job," Nikki said. "You don't happen to have an hourly rate, do you?"

"Ha," I said. "Okay, well. Thanks for dropping by. I have to get back to work now."

Nikki held up one hand like a crossing guard. "Wait. I've got some potential buyers for your house. They'll have to see the inside first, of course, but we've already done a drive-by and it's just what they're looking for. They're in a rush though, so we'll need to move fast. I was hoping I could bring them by tonight, as soon as Big Kevin gets home to watch the twins."

I closed my eyes. When I opened them again, she was still standing there.

"No," I said. "The timing is way off. And well, just no."

Behind her, Nikki Jr. and Kevin Jr. took off down the hallway like twin bats out of hell.

I pointed. As soon as Nikki turned around to look, I escaped to my classroom and shut the door behind me.

Thirteen

John answered his phone on the first ring. I loved that he wasn't the kind of guy who waited around for the second ring, or even the third, just so he wouldn't appear overeager to talk to me.

"So," I said. "Who was your first teacher that you can remember?"

"Miss Bluffton," he said right away. "First grade. She had tall puffy hair and shoulders like a defensive lineman, and she passed out brand new eight-packs of crayons to the entire class on the first day of school."

"Aww," I said. "What a sweet memory."

"And then she walked up and down the aisles with a box and collected all the black crayons. She said it was a sad color."

"Oh, that's awful."

"Yeah, especially since it was a cigar box that, even to a first grader, seemed vaguely reminiscent of a coffin."

"Hmm," I said. "Maybe the truth was that she taught Goth kids at night and needed the black crayons for them. Or the vampire kids."

"Interesting theory," John said. "Although wouldn't the vampire kids have wanted our red crayons?"

John and Horatio were spending another week at John's place, so my plan was to start getting my house ready to sell while they were gone, on the off chance that John and I actually found a house to buy together in this lifetime. So far all I'd managed to do was watch a couple of HGTV episodes about purging your belongings and staging your house. It was a surprisingly satisfying television viewing experience, one that left me feeling like I'd made some progress on my own house, much the way flipping through a cookbook sometimes made me feel almost as if I'd done some cooking.

"Well," John said. "That short term executive rental agent called today. Apparently someone is champing at the bit to get into my condo. His company must be giving him a pretty big housing allowance, because he's even offered to increase the rent by a considerable amount. I know the timing is just off, but I have to tell you it's tempting."

"Must be something in the air," I said. "*Nikki* stopped by my classroom after school today to say she might have potential buyers for my house. They've already done a drive-by, of course. To tell you the truth, I think it's all just an elaborate ploy so she can get inside to see what a sloppy housekeeper *Big Kevin's* starter wife is."

"I've still got the business card she gave me," John said. "Do you want me to give her a call in the morning and see what's up? I mean, I can understand you not wanting to deal with her, but I don't have an issue with it. Unless we find out she's married to my ex, too."

"Thanks," I said. "But what would be the point? My house isn't even close to being ready to sell. Though I did just finish watching a compelling episode of *Staging Wars*."

My doorbell rang.

"Somebody's at my door," I said. "Weird—nobody ever comes over this late. Except for my family, of course, but they've all managed to figure out where I hide the key, so they usually just walk right in."

"Make sure you check first before you open the door."

"Will do," I said. "Hang on."

Once you get to a certain age, pretty much everything reminds you of something that has happened before. As I walked down the hallway to my front door, I flashed back to a night when John and I were first fumbling our way toward each other. My doorbell had rung, and just like now I'd asked him to stay on the line so I could see who it was. I'd looked through my peephole to find a pink scalp peering up at me through teased and hair-sprayed blond hair. It was Dolly, arguably my father's craziest girlfriend of them all. She'd barged in, hung up on John, commandeered my couch. John had come to my rescue. And the rest was history.

In full déjà vu mode, I stood on my tiptoes and peeked out the peephole. But instead of my father's old girlfriend, I found myself looking at my wasband's new wife.

"Speak of the devil," I whispered into my cell. "It's Nikki. And she's got a couple with her. I can't believe she had the nerve to show up when I specifically told her no. I'm just going to pretend I'm not home. Wait, you don't think she knows how to pick locks, do you?"

"Now might be a good time for me to call her," John said, coming to my rescue once again.

. . . . .

John and Horatio made great time getting to my place. I'd spent the forty-five minutes or so while they were in the car running around my house, faux-cleaning like a maniac. I'd relocated my dirty clothes from the floor to a laundry basket and lugged it out to my car. I'd carried another laundry basket into the bathroom and filled it until it was just short of over-flowing. I didn't want my wasband's wife to know anything about me, not even what kind of deodorant or mascara I used.

I was out of laundry baskets at this point, so I found a cardboard box in the garage and walked around my house with it, throwing in every single personal item I could find, including my prenatal vitamins. And the rabbit ears.

I rummaged through a pile of scrapbooks on the bottom shelf of my office. I pulled out my wedding album, dusted it off with one hand, held it for a moment, slid it into the box under the rabbit ears so they didn't get bent. No matter what Nikki might have thought if she'd found it while snooping around, the fact that I hadn't yet ditched my wedding album wasn't at all about not letting go of my wasband. My plan was that one of these days I was going to get around to taking a Photoshop class and then I'd edit him out of every single picture. Minus Kevin, there were some great photos in that album.

I circled back to my bedroom where I dumped my fairly pathetic collection of bras and underwear into the box, too, then opened my lingerie drawer. I liked the concept of lingerie, but I had to admit I never seemed to get around to actually wearing it. I pulled out a satiny black slip-like little number that I must have picked up in an optimistic moment, yanked off its tags, draped it casually across my bed. I took a step back. It was a good look. I'd have to consider making my bed more often, too.

I went back to my lingerie drawer and pulled out another piece that had never been test-driven, this one in black lace. I yanked off its tags on my way to the bathroom, hung it on the hook on the inside of the door. Then I stuffed both sets of tags into the pocket of my jeans so I didn't leave any lack-of-wearing evidence behind.

I dumped the final item in my lingerie drawer into the box. It was a pink feather boa, one end slightly chewed by Mother Teresa, my brother Michael's St. Bernard—long story. Then I jammed the box in next to the laundry baskets in the backseat of my car.

I didn't have time to vacuum, so I made a quick run-through with my blow dryer turned on high, plugging it in wherever I found an open outlet, propelling accumulated dust and beach sand under the nearest rug or piece of furniture.

I had to admit that it worked pretty well. If I ever got sick of teaching, maybe I could get my own HGTV show on fake cleaning. I'd have to research the demographics, but I bet the potential audience would be huge.

When headlights lit up my driveway, I waited until I was sure it was John and Horatio and not Nikki. I grabbed a few treats from the treat jar for Horatio and met them in the front yard.

As soon as Horatio finished peeing on my grass, John handed me his end of the leash and Horatio's travel water bowl.

I gave John a quick kiss. "Thank you. Call me the second they're gone."

"Will do."

"What exactly did you tell Nikki anyway?" I asked.

"Just that you were out for the evening, but I could meet her at your house." John pulled out his cell, woke it up. "In exactly six minutes."

I gave Horatio a treat. "Okay, we're out of here. Whatever you do, don't let her out of your sight long enough to do any snooping."

Horatio and I found a parking spot near the town pier. We strolled up and down Marshbury's Main Street, Horatio stopping to lift his leg at every vertical surface we passed. The sidewalks weren't quite rolled up for the night yet, the air was crisp but not cold, the scent of low tide was almost strong enough to taste.

A sky full of stars sparkled above us. I wished on the first one I saw. It was a vague wish—for a house of some kind, and a family of some sort, and whole uninterrupted days and weeks and months spent with John.

Fourteen

"Noooo," I said the next morning when my alarm went off. "I barely slept a wink."

"I know," John said. "I didn't sleep much either. I couldn't stop turning it all over and over in my head." He pushed the covers off, swung his legs over the side of the bed. "Why don't you jump in the shower while I start the coffee." He leaned over and picked up my black satin bed-staging lingerie from the floor. "And if you come out wearing this, I'll even cook breakfast."

I pulled the covers up to my chin. "Ha. If I come out wearing that, we won't have time for breakfast. *And* I'll be late for school."

John walked around to my side of the bed and leaned over for a kiss. "What's interesting to me is that

I've never seen this before. Or that lace thing hanging in the bathroom either."

"I've been saving them," I said, "for when the rabbit ears lose their luster."

By the time I made it out to the kitchen, showered and dressed for work, the coffee was brewed and John was flipping two eggs in a frying pan.

I poured myself a cup of coffee. "This I could get used to."

John tilted the frying pan, and two perfectly fried eggs slid right on to a plate.

"Impressive," I said.

He handed me the plate. "So this is breakfast: egg. Unless you'd like to accompany it with the expired yogurt that's in your refrigerator."

"No thanks. But to be fair, I'm pretty sure I have some stale cereal in the cupboard, too. And I only threw out my English muffins because they were turning green."

John cracked two more eggs into the frying pan while I topped off his coffee. John and his eggs joined me at my little kitchen table, and Horatio crawled under and curled up at John's feet. I checked the time on my microwave clock, realized I had a full twelve minutes before I needed to race out the door to school.

"Yum," I said. "This is really civilized. I almost forgot how to eat breakfast sitting down."

John took a bite of egg, looked at me.

"Okay," I said. "I still think you spending the day house-hunting with Nikki is completely insane."

John reached for his coffee. "We've been over and over this, Sarah. We've got a tenant for my condo. We've got buyers for your house—"

"Possible buyers," I said. "I mean, it's not like there's been an offer."

"But if it happens, we'll have to move fast. And if Nikki represents your sale and also helps us find a house, she's already said she'll work with us on her percentage, which will make it a win-win."

I rolled my eyes. "There is no win-win when it comes to working with your ex-husband's wife."

"Think about it." John leaned forward, in full selling mode. "You'd be completely bypassing the stress of having to get your place ready or even to officially put it on the market."

I sighed. "The other way to look at it is that if we both have interest in our places without even trying, it will happen again once we're ready. So there's no need to jump on some kind of lowball offer from *Nikki*, assuming she even manages to get one."

John reached under the table to give Horatio a pat, and Horatio's tail thumped against my ankle. John stood up, took the three steps necessary to get across my tiny kitchen and grab the coffee pot. "It's my time and I'm willing to take the risk. I'll get some work done between now and when I'm supposed to meet her. And then I'll spend a whirlwind day with her looking at houses."

"What about Horatio?"

"I'll give your dad a call and see if he can at least come by and take him out for a walk while I'm gone. If he's too busy, I'll get him to give me the number of Bark & Roll Forever—it would be a good way to check them out. Bottom line, doing it this way will spare you from spending a day with Nikki. And if anything looks promising, the two of us can take a look at it tonight."

"You mean the three of us, don't you?" I finished my last bite of egg, reached for my coffee. "I keep telling you—I don't want anything to do with Nikki. I still think she's just trying to butt into my life. Which is hardly a *win-win*, John."

A text beeped in to John's phone. He put the coffee pot back, picked up the phone from the counter.

He looked up from his phone. "You've got an offer."

"Oh, please," I said. "How much?"

John put his hand on my shoulder, held his phone in front of my face.

"Holy shit," I said.

He nodded. "That's a pretty strong offer."

I took his phone from him, looked at the number again to be sure I wasn't hallucinating. "That's like saying the Hulk is a pretty strong guy. Who in their right minds would pay that much money for a ranchburger?"

"We've seen what's out there. This is a solid house in a great neighborhood that's essentially move-in ready and also has lots of potential for upgrading."

I tried to wrap my brain around what John was saying, but all I could think of was how pissed off Kevin would be when he found out how big the offer was. In a way, especially if you factored out Nikki's commission, you could look at it that I got the last laugh.

John was still talking. "And not to get all metaphysical here, but I think when the universe starts sending everything you're asking for in your direction, you've got to either jump on it or admit that you might not really want it after all."

I resisted the urge to grab a pen and a piece of paper so I could write that down. "That's not true," I said instead. "Of course I want to buy a house with you."

John sat down again.

We looked at each other across my tiny table.

"Okay, this is the best I can do," I said. "If the universe sends you and Nikki to the perfect house today, we'll talk."

. . . . .

Once the students had all arrived, I looked around for Polly so we could start gathering the kids for circle time. I heard our toilet flush, the sink spigot turn on. Eventually Polly came out of our classroom bathroom looking green around the gills.

I headed in her direction, stopped what I hoped was a safe distance away. "Oh, no," I whispered. "You can't get sick on me this early in the year."

She swallowed carefully. "It must have been something I ate last night."

"Do you want me to see if there's any ginger ale in the teacher's room?"

"No, really, I'm fine. I think I just need something in my stomach." She opened our snack cabinet, poured a few Goldfish into her hand, popped one in her mouth.

"Okay," I said. "But let me know if you need to go home. The office can try to get a substitute for the rest of the day, and in the meantime I can ask Ethan and June to keep the door between our classrooms open."

Polly was already placing the nametags in front of the appropriate dots on our classroom circle. I made a peace sign and walked around waving my hand slowly back and forth to get everybody's attention. Then I took my seat at the circle, still holding up my two fingers. The kids made peace signs, too, and joined me.

After we'd gathered, one empty dot remained right next to the nametag with a picture of a school bus on it.

"Where's Depp?" I said.

We all looked around the classroom as if we were playing a riveting game of I Spy with My Little Eye.

Five-year-old Millicent pointed across the room. "I found him!"

Depp was sound asleep in the reading boat, his school slipper-clad feet resting on one of the wooden seats and his head all but buried in the pile of pillows on the bottom of the boat.

Polly started to get up, but I beat her to it. I tucked a pillow under Depp's head to make sure he didn't suffocate, then grabbed *Bats on the Beach* from one of the shelves.

Depp kicked his feet hard, just missing me. "I don't wanna walk," he yelled in his sleep. "I wanna take the alligator."

The kids burst out laughing. "Elevator," I enunciated clearly as I walked back to our circle. "If you don't take the stairs, you take the elevator. Or the escalator."

Once the hilarity died down, I read *Bats on the Beach*, turning the book to face the kids after I finished each page and making a measured swoop from side to side so they could all see the illustrations. We'd read *Stellaluna* yesterday, and tomorrow we'd read *Brooms Are For Flying*. We were spreading out our Halloween fun over the entire month of October so the kids could savor it instead of shoveling it all into one jam-packed and overwhelming day of celebration.

After I finished reading, I put the book back on the shelf in the reading boat. Then I grabbed the bat puppets the kids had already decorated with paint and wiggly eyes. Polly pushed herself up to help me pass them out. I thought her color was a little bit better now, but maybe I just wanted it to be.

Once bats were on fingers all around, I started singing to the tune of "Mary Had a Little Lamb":

Mary had a little bat, little bat, little bat.
Mary had a little bat, its wings were black as night.
It flew up in the air one day, air one day, air one day.
It flew up in the air one day,
and disappeared from sight.

Polly and the kids jumped in, following right along. We danced our bat finger puppets back and forth, made them fly up over our heads, and on the final line of the verse we hid our bats behind our backs. I wasn't a brilliant songwriter, but as long as I stuck to a song that we all knew, I could pretty much rewrite it to suit any holiday. I'd spent more Saturday nights than I cared to remember sitting around all by myself with a notebook and a pen repurposing songs for my classroom.

We moved on to the next verse:

Mary had a little bat, little bat, little bat.
Mary had a little bat, sleeping upside down.
It followed her to school one day, school one day,
school one day.
It followed her to school one day,
and turned into a clown.

"I hate clowns," Depp screamed from the reading boat.

"Me, too," somebody else screamed. The sentiment spread around the circle like a wave at a baseball game. Four-year-old Annie sobbed in high drama. Three-year-old Josiah patted her back.

As Depp staggered over to us, his thumb in his mouth and his hair sticking out randomly, I made a mental note to change *turned into a clown* to *went out on the town* the next the time we sang the song.

Depp ignored his school bus nametag and his dot and went right for Polly's lap. Polly hugged him and smoothed his hair down while I collected the bats. I put them away and headed for our CD player. Then I cranked up the volume and motioned for everybody to stand up.

By the time we finished freeze dancing our way through "Ghostbusters," all signs of clown phobia had vanished. Depp was laughing and busting moves along with the rest of the kids. Polly was no longer ghostly pale.

I was feeling pretty good, too, and I'd almost managed to take my mind off the fact that John Anderson was spending the day with my wasband's wife.

Fifteen

It wasn't every day that I arrived home from school to find a pink ice cream truck parked in my driveway. In fact, it wasn't any day up until this one.

Just as I was reaching for my doorknob, my father opened my front door. He was wearing a hot pink T-shirt that said BARK & ROLL FOREVER.

"Come on in and take a load off," he said.

"Gee, thanks," I said. "Nice shirt."

My father threw his shoulders back so I could get a better look. "The gals offered to order me up one in another color, but I told them not to bother. I've always profaned that it takes a manly man to pull off pink."

"Well, you're certainly that," I said even though, profaning aside, in all the years I'd spent with my father, I'd never once heard him even acknowledge the existence of the color pink. "And besides, you wouldn't want to clash with the ice cream truck."

Belatedly, Horatio sprinted down my hallway, barking his head off. The hot pink bandanna around his neck also said BARK & ROLL FOREVER.

"Some watchdog you are." I dropped my big canvas teacher's bag to the floor and squatted down to give him a pat. "And you're totally rockin' the pink, too."

"Homer and I need to get back to work," my dad said. "We just stopped by to use the facilities. But I suppose we might be able to make time for a quick cup of tea if you've already got the kettle on."

Given that I'd barely made it into my hallway, it was highly doubtful that I'd had time to put the kettle on, but this was the kind of logic that always escaped my father.

"Sure," I said. "I think it's almost boiling."

I fired up the burner under my teakettle, found the tea bags and mugs. When Kevin moved out, he'd taken all the coffee mugs with him excerpt for four that had been gifts from my students. Since John and I had already used VIRGINIA IS FOR LOVERS and I LUV MY TEACHER at breakfast this morning, that left FAVORITE TEACHER and TEACH PEACE for my father and me.

My dad helped himself to the contents of the jar on my counter, threw a treat up in the air. Horatio caught it before it hit the ground.

"Sit," my father said.

Horatio sat. I decided to wait until after I'd poured the tea.

"That's a good fella," my father said. "Help me reel in a few more customers before we call it quits for the day, and there's more where that came from."

I leaned back against the counter. "Thanks for helping John out with Horatio today, Dad. I have to say your newfound love of dogs couldn't have come at a more convenient time."

"I don't think of Homer as a dog. In fact, I'm training him up to be my wing man." My father opened my fridge, closed it again.

"I've got some stale cereal if you're desperate," I said.

"I can wait. The girls have one of the coolers in the truck all stocked up with the good old ice cream treats. They've got the other cooler filled to the brim with bone-shaped pooch treats tied up with some kind of frou-frou pink ribbons and little business cards. Homer had a hard time sharing in the beginning, and I was worried about him being a bit of a lollygagger, but he's shaping up just fine."

The teakettle whistled. I poured us each a cup and joined my dad at the kitchen table.

"Well," I said. "It certainly sounds like your new job's going well."

"That it is, that it is." My father nodded, dipped his tea bag up and down in the water. "I just hope it doesn't turn into a cat fight when the ladies find out I'm dating all of them."

"Da-ad."

My father laughed, raked back the hunk of thick white hair that was always falling into his eyes, slapped his knee. "Just yanking your chain, honey, just yanking your chain. Truth be told I'm holding out for the leader of the pack—that Betty Ann is one choice bit of calico."

. . . . .

I knew I should have stayed home, at the very least to unpack the laundry baskets and the big cardboard box that so far had only made it from the backseat of my car to my bedroom floor. But how often does life hand you a chance to ride shotgun in an ice cream truck?

As we drove, our speakers blasted out "Leader of the Pack" in that distinctive melodic chime of ice cream trucks everywhere. "Oh, this is so much fun," I said.

"Back in the day," my father said, "you used to have to crank up the chimes by hand to play a tune. But this baby's got the sound all rigged to run off engine power or some such thing."

The ice cream truck tunes of my childhood began playing in my head: "It's a Small World," "Pop Goes the Weasel," "Turkey in the Straw." An ice cream truck driving up our street on a hot summer's day would send all six Hurlihy kids running for their piggybanks. Or we'd hear one jangling away as it pulled into the beach parking lot, and we'd all gang up on our mother, begging for an advance on our allowances, promising to do extra chores, if only she'd please, please, please let us have a Big Dipper or a Cherry Bomb to soothe our sun and saltwater parched throats.

As if he'd seen my flashback, my father turned off the music and pulled into the nearest beach parking lot. He put the ice cream truck into park, left the engine running.

He jumped out, spry as ever, and swung open the back door. By the time I caught up with him he was pulling out a hot pink carpet runner and some metal poles with thick pink cords attached to them. I helped him roll out the carpet, which was sprinkled randomly with black paw prints, so that it created a path to the service window. We set up a row of cords on either side of the carpet.

"That Betty Ann is one smart cookie," my father said. "This arrangement not only keeps your customers orderly, but it gets 'em all charged up like they're lining up for a Hollywood movie premiere."

I contemplated the idea of asking to borrow the runner and poles to try them out on my students. Getting a roomful of preschoolers to line up for anything is always a challenge.

My dad climbed up on a stool, unlatched the service counter from the side of the truck, pulled it down until it was horizontal to the ground. Then he swung out a stop sign-shaped sign so you could read BARK & ROLL FOREVER from both sides.

He wiggled his bushy white eyebrows. "The original lettering underneath says DON'T SKID ON A KID, but the girls covered it up for business purposes."

"Good thinking," I said.

We climbed back into the truck. My father turned the music on again, cranked up the volume, worked his way between the two front seats so he could slide open the service window.

"Homer and I will hand out the pooch treats and cards," he said. "You can sell the ice cream. Cash only, and the two of us split the tips right down the middle. Homer takes his pay in kibble."

"Deal," I said. We sealed it with a high five.

Dogs weren't allowed to set paw on Marshbury beaches between 9 A.M. and 6 P.M. from the Friday before Memorial Day through the Monday of Labor Day weekend. But after Labor Day, canines ruled the Marshbury beaches. Technically the dogs were supposed to be attached at all times to leashes held by the humans who accompanied them. But by this time in October, owners often let the rules slide long enough for their dogs to enjoy a quick burst of delicious late afternoon freedom.

Before I'd even opened the cash box, a gang of dogs was racing toward us, their leash-carrying owners hot on their heels. Word was clearly out about the pink ice cream truck's canine cargo—it was like being in one of those Disney movies where the dogs howl the news from dog to dog all across town.

A Jack Russell terrier with a jeweled collar managed to jump up high enough to make eye contact through the service window.

"Hold your horses, young lady," my father said. He opened the cooler and grabbed a handful of treat cards.

A Great Dane stood on its hind legs and rested its front paws on the service counter.

"Uh-uh-uh, we'll have none of that pushy business," my father said. "Find someone who can read and has opposable thumbs to untie the ribbon on this baby for you, and we'll be in business."

Eventually the humans caught up and my dad started handing out cards and treats while he talked up Bark & Roll Forever. He joked, he flirted. I sold the occasional ice cream.

"Billy Boy Hurlihy's still got it," my father said once the crowd had moved on.

I gave Horatio a treat and started unwrapping a Nutty Buddy for myself. "You sure do."

My dad grabbed a Toasted Almond from the cooler. Horatio began barking like crazy.

"Sorry about that, chief," my father said. "A little jaunt after each stop is a part of the deal, and this one doesn't let me get away with forgetting, I'll give him that."

We put everything away, locked up the ice cream truck, strolled up a long narrow boardwalk toward the beach. The sun was low over the marsh behind us, an orange ball trailing pink and blue horizontal stripes as it dropped. The tide was almost high, more beach disappearing with every wave or two. My dad and I leaned up against a big boulder in front of the seawall while Horatio went to work digging a hole.

I took a deep breath of salt air.

"So," my father said as he lapped his Toasted Almond. "I was talking to that fellow of yours about your situation when I picked up Homer."

"What situation?" I turned my Nutty Buddy side-ways so I could peel off a strip of nutty chocolate with my teeth, just like I used to do a gazillion years ago on this very same beach.

My father gestured with his ice cream bar as he spoke. "If you want my best advice, I'd say the two of you need to unload your pads quick while the ironing board is still hot."

After a lifetime of listening to my father butcher sayings, that actually made sense to me.

"You can both bunk in with me," my father continued. "And Homer, too, of course, as long as he doesn't try to take over my new recliner once you kids pony up for it."

Horatio looked up at the mention of his non-name, went back to digging.

I shivered. It was hard to say whether it was from the combination of the setting sun and the ice cream, or from the thought of moving in with my father. I put up the hood on my jacket, went back to my Nutty Buddy. "Thanks, Dad, but we wouldn't want to cramp your style."

"You wouldn't be cramping my style one single scin-tilla. The truth of the matter is that there are entire rooms I haven't set foot in since your mother . . ."

His voice trailed off. I tried not to let my eyes tear up.

My dad sighed. "It's a lot of house for one person to rattle around in. It might be a good thing to have some company again, even for a short spell." He draped an arm around me. "And besides, I could use a wee bit of design assistance on my man cavern. That new fella of yours has a good head on his shoulders."

My sigh came out sounding exactly like my father's. "We might not even need a place to stay. The offer on my house could fall through. Or the tenant for John's condo could change his mind. Or we might actually luck out and find a house to—"

"We'll need a few ground rules though. The first of which being that when I invite Betty Ann over for a romantic intermission in front of that new 72-inch flat screen, I'll expect the three of you to skedaddle until I give you the all clear to come back."

CHAPTER

Sixteen

As soon as he heard John's car in the driveway, Horatio went crazy, his nails scraping my front door like every teacher's nightmare, those proverbial fingernails on the blackboard.

I clipped on his leash and opened my door while it was still in one piece.

When Horatio dragged me across the lawn to greet John, I had to do a quick hop and a skip to keep up with him. John ruffled Horatio's ears and then leaned over him to give me a kiss.

He handed me a stack of CDs.

"Thanks," I said. I bit my tongue so I didn't add, *Great, just what I needed: more stuff to pack.*

"Nikki asked me to give these to you. She knew they didn't belong to Kevin. She said it always bothered her that he still had them."

The hairs on the back of my neck stood up, and not in a good way. "If something like that ever happens again, do me a favor and, I don't know, just don't let it, okay?"

John shrugged. "I think she was just trying to be nice."

I handed the leash to John and walked back into my house.

John caught up to me in my kitchen. He was carrying some papers that looked suspiciously like a purchase and sales agreement.

"I wasn't sure if you might have had time to stop at the grocery store after school," he said, "so I didn't want to duplicate efforts."

"Grocery store," I said. "Which one is that again?"

He opened my fridge, closed it again. "Takeout it is. How would you feel about salad and a Panini of some kind?"

"Pizza, subs, or marginal Chinese food," I said. "I hate to break it to you, but that's the extent of delivery round these here parts."

"Pizza it is," John said. "I'll call it in. Everything but anchovies is good for me."

"Broccoli and spinach," I said.

"Perfect," he said.

I put the teakettle on while John placed the order. Then we arranged ourselves at opposite sides of my kitchen table.

John broke the silence. "Well, we saw one house that I think could possibly work, but it needs quite a bit of work, and I'm not sure we could live in it during the renovations, especially if I'm trying to work remote."

My teakettle let out an angry whistle. I pushed myself up to a standing position. Sighed at the thought of having to hand wash two of my four mugs just to make tea. Found two clean wine glasses in my cabinet and decided it was a meant-to-be. So I opened one of the decoy Two Buck Chuck bottles on my counter and poured.

"Thanks," John said when I plopped our glasses down on the table. He sniffed his wine cautiously, raised his glass. "To staying the course."

I barely tapped his glass with mine. I watched him take a small sip, scrunch his eyes closed and make a face, swallow.

I took a deep breath. "What you said earlier about Nikki? And I quote: 'I think she was just trying to be nice.'"

John waited.

"A person who walked away with your former husband is not a nice person," I said. "Not that the former husband isn't ultimately responsible for being walk away-able, but still. Nice women don't do that to other women."

John tilted his head the way Horatio sometimes did when he was attempting to figure out a command. "And we need her to be a nice person because . . . ?"

"It's not that we need her to be a nice person," I said. "It's more that because she's not, we don't want to reward her for what she did. Or maybe it's that she doesn't deserve the privilege of having anything to do with us."

John took another small sip of wine. "People do a lot of stupid things. And you could also look at it that this particular stupid thing led to me meeting you, so while I'm sorry that you had to go through all that, I like the karmic result. So I say we forget about who deserves what, and get that tenant moved in to my condo and unload your house."

I shook my head. "But then what? I don't want to rush into buying a house just for the sake of buying it."

"So we look for a rental. Or we move in with your father until we find the right place."

"Moving in with my dad would be insane," I said. "I mean, I'm used to my family, but you have no idea what it would be like. They'd drive you absolutely crazy in a week. A week-and-a-half tops."

John shrugged. "I'd be fine. It would be short term, and it would keep us from getting all tied up in a rental contract. And if things get bad, it would give us even more incentive to find a house fast."

"No way," I said.

"Okay, then. That means we either have to find a rental or a house to buy."

"Fine," I said. "As long as we don't have to work with Nikki."

John shook his head. "We've got to move quickly. Nikki's motivated and she knows what we're looking for. And she's also planning to swing by to pick up the signed paperwork for the sale of your house tonight."

"Great."

Maybe I should have said something more. Or maybe John should have said something more. Or maybe we both just should have thought the whole thing through a little longer.

But I signed and dated the purchase and sales agreement. And then I took a long slug of Two Buck Chuck.

. . . . .

I'd barely gotten home from school the next day when Nikki pulled into my driveway."

"Geez," I said. "You don't think she's stalking me, do you?"

"Come on," John said. "Let's focus on finding a house."

I climbed into the backseat of Nikki's monstrous SUV so John would have to sit up front.

"Just unbuckle the car seats and throw them into the way back," Nikki said, like that wouldn't have involved a Herculean effort. Instead, I wedged myself into the vacant seat between the twin car seats. Stray Cheerios crunched as I sat on them, and something sharper threatened to do more serious damage. I reached under one thigh and pulled out a plastic dinosaur, which I immediately identified it as a brachiosaurus. Reached under my other thigh and found a triceratops. I placed one on each car seat, resisted the urge to buckle them in.

"Here we go," Nikki said as she backed out of my driveway and handed John a pile of papers at the same time. I checked to make sure my own seatbelt was buckled. "You can be my co-pilot. Pull up that foreclosure listing, the one with the cute little note the house wrote."

"*So let me tell you the truth,*" John read. "*I lost my kitchen in a poker game. My old owners also had a hard time letting go of things, so they took my toilet and dual vanities with them when they left. But look on the bright side, I'll appreciate your TLC ever so much, and you won't have to tear me apart before you give me a makeover. I'm AS IS, but aren't we all if you stop to think about it. I have tremendous potential, if I do say so myself. And I simply know that I won't last long!*"

"Isn't that the cutest thing ever?" Nikki said.

"Sure," I said, "if you like depressing first-person house stories."

"A blank canvas might not be a bad place to start," John said.

The first thing I noticed when Nikki pulled into the driveway was that the house had a detached garage, not what you're hoping for when you live in a snowy climate.

"Hmm," I said as I noticed the second thing. "When it was writing its note, the house must have forgotten to mention that the owners took the garage door, too."

"That's really just cosmetic," Nikki said. "A new garage door will hardly cost you anything."

Apparently the owners hadn't had a problem letting go of their dirty dishes. They were piled high in both halves of the sink. It looked like someone must have added soap and water to let them soak a few months ago and then forgotten about it.

"But look on the bright side," I said. "I'll make you feel great about your own lack of housekeeping skills!"

"Big Kevin always says you had the best sense of humor," Nikki said.

"Wow, what's that?" John said, possibly to cut me off before I said anything even more hilarious. He pointed to a circular hole that looked like it had been hacked in the hardwood floor with an ax.

"Ice fishing?" I said.

"I've got a great floor guy," Nikki said. "I'll give you his card."

Permanent marker had been scribbled all over the walls like graffiti. Most of it was abstract, but there were also a few choice words that made it clear that the owners had not been happy campers when they left.

John opened the door to the basement. "Whoa. It looks like they just threw everything in the entire house down here. I don't think we can even get down the stairs."

"Come on," I said. "Let's get out of here. This place has seriously bad vibes."

We went through more houses than I thought would be possible in a single evening. One had a note saying that the family hamster had escaped and if we happened to see it, we should know that IT IS NOT A MOUSE.

Even though it was supposed to be empty, there was a guy asleep in a bed in another house, the covers pulled up to his chin. We all backed out of the room carefully and got out of there fast.

The final house we saw was an estate sale. The elderly owner had died recently and her out-of-town heirs were selling. The rooms were small and dark and the walls were an explosion of floral wallpaper.

"It's not officially on the market," Nikki said. "But we just got the listing so I'm sneaking us in a little early."

The bed was unmade in one of the tiny bedrooms. A book and glasses sat on the night table.

I joined John in the infinitesimal hallway bathroom, where a set of false teeth was soaking in a glass on the sink.

"My Uncle Walt had a glass eye," John said. "When he used to visit when I was a kid, sometimes I'd find it in a glass by the bathroom sink in the middle of the night. It scared the shit out of me."

"Oh, you poor thing," I said, still eyeing the teeth, hoping they wouldn't start chattering on their own.

"Well, that's about it," Nikki said when we were back in her SUV again and I was wedged between the car seats.

"What about rentals?" John said.

Nikki shrugged. "I've looked. All you're going to get right now is a winter rental. Which means you're just going to have to turn around and move again in six or seven months."

Even I knew that the writing was on the wall, but that didn't make it any easier to admit.

"I hate to say it," I said, "but I think we need to move in with my father. Just for a little while until the right house comes along."

Seventeen

"It's dizzling," Jaden said as he stood by his hook and started wiggling out of his raincoat, which was bright green and had a hood like a frog's head.

"No it's not," Juliette said. "It's raining." Juliette was standing beside Jaden and taking off her raincoat, too. It was bright red and the hood had black polka dots with little ladybug wings sticking out. I had to admit their raincoats were making me wish for something a bit cheerier than the beige one I'd worn to school today, which I'd had for more years than I cared to count. Maybe once John and I got settled in at my father's house, I'd actually go out shopping and see if anybody made ladybug raincoats for adults.

"My mommy says it's *dizzling*," Jaden said.

"*My* mommy says it's spitting," Depp said. His raincoat was bright blue and covered with Dalmatians. And also fire trucks, which I hoped he wouldn't feel the need to mispronounce out loud.

Juliette rolled her eyes. "It's raining," she announced definitively. She had a pretty good eye roll going for a four-year-old.

Jaden gave her a little shove. "It's *dizzling.*"

"Ouch." Juliette crossed her arms over her chest. "You hurt my heart."

"Get used to it," Polly whispered to me as we separated the rain brigade and redirected them to more constructive activities.

The day passed slowly, as dizzly days often do. After a rollicking round of freeze dancing to "Purple People Eater," we got the kids seated at the long tables. Polly and I passed out clementines all around. The kids drew jack-o'-lantern faces on their clementines with markers as if they were tiny pumpkins, and then they peeled and ate them. The Ghost Smoothie Polly and I concocted by mixing bananas, almond milk, and vanilla yogurt in a blender was a big hit.

We relocated to our circle where I read *Room on the Broom*, about a witch with a flyaway hat. After I finished reading, we made up new yoga moves that recreated all the characters in the book: the witch, the striped cat, the dog that rescued the hat, the parrot, the frog, the red dragon that came along. The morning kids went home, and the full-day kids moved on to lunch and the rest of their day.

Eventually Polly and I were sitting in kid-size chairs across the table from each other, our calendar on the table between us, Polly in charge of the pen.

"Three good things and we're out of here till Monday," I said. "Okay, I'll start. Depp didn't say fire fuck once."

Polly wrote FF in small letters, circled it and drew a line through it.

"Nobody poked an eye out with an umbrella," Polly said. She drew an open umbrella with a smiley face on it.

I flashed back to John's uncle, hoped he hadn't lost his eye when he was in preschool.

"Juliette's hurt heart healed quickly," I said.

Polly drew a heart with a big J on it and then added lines radiating out from the heart like rays from the sun.

She sighed. "I think hearts heal a lot faster when you're four."

. . . . .

By morning all signs of spitting, dizzling and raining were gone, and John and I were standing in front of the Marshbury storage unit we'd rented.

"This kind of thing looks like a lot more fun on *Storage Wars*," I said.

"Yeah, there's a real sadness to these places," John said. "It's like you can feel it in the air—all the upheaval in people's lives, the way they dropped everything off in a hurry, hoping they'd be back to pick it up again before they knew it . . ."

"Whoa," I said. "And to think you're supposed to be the cheery one in this relationship."

John was renting his condo fully furnished. He'd boxed up his personal items and anything else he didn't want to leave behind. I'd traded my car for my sister Carol's minivan for the day so we could move whatever he didn't need right away to the storage unit.

John had hired professional movers who specialized in antiques to move his two pinball machines, one an authentic The Addams Family model, which according to John was the most popular pinball machine of all time, and the other an Eight Ball Deluxe. When we first met, John was winding down a financially unproductive stint as a vintage pinball machine restorer. "It seems," he'd said, "that I have the soul of a pinball wizard but the brain of an accountant. Essentially, it's the existential struggle of my life."

I'd yet to figure out what the existential struggle of my own life was, and I still didn't quite get the allure of pinball machines, but I knew the two he'd held on to meant a lot to John. He'd decided they were too valuable to leave in his condo while it was being rented. So we'd gone back and forth and back and forth about whether it was safer to keep them in a locked storage unit, where anything might happen, or in my family's house, where anything could definitely happen.

In the end, John decided that if the pinball machines stayed with us at my dad's house, it would be easier to keep an eye on them.

"Which leaves the larger question," I said. "If we're busy keeping an eye on the pinball machines, who's going to keep an eye on my father?"

John finished reading the instructions that had come with our storage unit. "Okay, here goes." He pushed in the combination, unlocked the padlock, opened the garage-like door of our storage unit to reveal an interior that looked like an oversize cement jail cell. The cement floor was topped with a layer of wooden planking.

"Home sweet home," I said. "Let's remember to leave some space for a mattress just in case things get really bad at my dad's house."

"I sure hope this place lives up to the promise of being climate-controlled." John opened the minivan's rear door, grabbed a box.

I managed to pick up a neatly labeled but ridiculously heavy cardboard box labeled BOOKS and staggered behind John into the storage unit.

Once we'd emptied Carol's minivan of all but a scattering of toys, a few headless dolls, some empty water bottles, and a plethora of assorted snack crumbs, we moved on to unloading John's Acura. Before we knew it, columns of evenly stacked boxes filled the back end of the storage unit.

I rubbed my lower back with both hands. "As my father and Amos 'n' Andy like to say, oh, my aching sacro-crackerjack. But, wow, we're actually doing this."

"Yes. We. Are." John reached into his trunk one more time, clicked it closed. He handed me a paper bag.

My stomach growled, hoping for food. I reached into the bag and pulled out a can of paint.

"Thanks," I said. "How romantic."

John grinned. "Hey, you're the one who nixed the idea of an engagement ring."

"I don't want an engagement ring," I said. "It'll only remind me of the perfectly good one that's sitting in my junk drawer. And you know that's why I don't want the whole wedding thing either—anything we do or don't do will trigger flashbacks to our first weddings."

"I can see that to a certain degree. But I still don't understand why we can't get settled in at your dad's house and then elope. We can use cigar bands for the rings if it will make you feel better." He opened his Heath Bar eyes wide. "Vegas, baby."

"Ha," I said. "You're so not a Vegas, baby kind of guy."

"Then what about Scotland? I've done some Googling, and you need to submit the documents and fees fifteen days ahead of time, but it's much easier for foreigners to get a marriage license in Scotland than in most of Europe. Or we could make it simple and take a quick trip to Florida. There's no waiting period on marriage licenses for out-of-state couples in Florida. Or what about—"

"Come on, John. We've already been through all this. We don't need another headache right now. We've got enough going on between looking for a house and trying to have a . . ." I couldn't quite say the B word.

John put his hands on my shoulders, gave me a kiss on my forehead. "Where are we?"

I blew out a puff of air. "I think I'm close to ovulating. So I'm off the occasional glass of Two Buck Chuck and back on fulltime seltzer just in case."

He nodded, started to say something optimistic, reined it in.

"I can't handle worrying about one more thing," I said. "When we're settled into our new place together, and when the other part has played out one way or the other, we can figure out the marriage piece."

"Maybe we could invite everyone over for a house-warming party and surprise them with a wedding? My parents would need a little bit of notice, and my sister would, too—"

"Please?" I closed my eyes, opened them again. "So, about that paint."

John cleared his throat. "In Scotland, homeowners paint their front doors red after paying off their mortgages. A little factoid I ran into when I found myself taking a slight detour on the Internet."

I stretched out the hand still holding the paint can so I could read the label. "Million Dollar Red. Great name for a paint color. And it's a cool idea, except that I haven't paid off my mortgage yet."

"If we wait until the buyers own your house to paint it, at the very least it would be trespassing. And possibly desecration of property."

"But if we paint it now," I said, "it might jinx the sale. And what if the new owners don't like red front doors?"

"Then we'll paint it back for them. Come on, I think it'll be a nice way to mark the occasion."

"Okay," I said. "But only if you promise to wear a kilt."

Eighteen

John and I ate Maria's subs on my front steps in the late afternoon sun, Horatio curled up at our feet waiting for one of us to drop a potato chip. Then we took my door off its hinges and laid it out on the front lawn, using some stray bricks a sadly kilt-less John had found in my garage to keep it up off the grass.

Horatio whined softly from the other side of the screened door where he'd been banished so he wouldn't leave paw prints in the paint.

It felt strange to be painting the front door of a house I'd already accepted an offer on, but also oddly therapeutic. We stroked our Million Dollar Red-loaded foam brushes over the boring black paint Kevin and I had never gotten around to changing. John's brush strokes were measured and precise, mine a lot less so.

I remembered the high hopes I'd had when Kevin and I first moved in here. For our house, for our marriage, for our lives. How painful it had been to watch it all fall apart, inch by inch, until there didn't seem to be enough left to salvage. Even at the time I'd known I could have tried harder, but I couldn't seem to make myself do it.

I tucked my hair behind my ears, wished I'd thought to pull it back into a stubby ponytail. We started in on the second coat of paint, right over the first.

"So," I said. "There was this column called 'Can This Marriage Be Saved?' in one of the women's magazines. I think it was *Ladies Home Journal.* Anyway, my mother had a subscription, and I used to read it every month, before I even had a boyfriend, trying to store up all the solutions in my memory banks in case I ever needed them. When things started falling apart between Kevin and me, I actually thought about sending in a letter. I used to wake up in the middle of the night and try to compose it in my head, even though I wasn't sure whether or not the column existed anymore."

John did that head-tilting thing again.

I shrugged. "I know it probably wouldn't have made any difference. But don't you ever look back and think that you could have tried harder?"

"Sure. I think you can always try harder."

I looked down at my red paint-spattered hands. John's were completely paint-free.

"What if this doesn't work?" I said.

"We'll make it work," John said. "Whatever happens, we'll try harder."

We leaned across my door and kissed on it.

"Let's talk about something cheery," John said. "Either that or I could let you in on the fact that you've just become a Million Dollar Redhead."

"Great." I started to reach for my hair, realized I'd only make it worse. "Okay, I can do cheery if I focus. What was your favorite treat from the ice cream truck when you were a kid?"

A wave of sadness broke over John's face. "I don't know. My parents told me that the ice cream truck only played music when it was out of ice cream."

"Oh, that's so awful. I'm not sure I even want to meet your parents now. Why do adults say things like that?"

"I think they probably just wanted me to eat my spinach so I'd grow up big and strong like Popeye." He bent his elbow and squeezed his fist to show me his bicep.

"Impressive," I said. But the truth was that I wanted to give him back that portion of his childhood, the part where he could dash across the parking lot to the sound of an ice cream truck knowing that a ridiculously unhealthy treat he'd never forget the taste of was waiting for him.

I wrapped the used brushes in the crumpled paper from our subs and stuffed the whole mess into the paper bag. John put the lid back on the paint can.

"So," he said. "I think I'd better try to get my last few boxes packed. Do you want to take the ride with me?"

I looked at the shiny red front door still sprawled across my lawn. "I should get some packing done, too. And that way we can give the door more drying time. When you get back, we can rehang the door and then I'll return Carol's minivan and get my car."

"Okay, I'll pick up some kind of exotic urban takeout for dinner and bring it back with me." John opened the screen door. "How 'bout you, pal. Do you want to come along?"

Horatio didn't need to be asked twice. He jumped up, covered John's face with kisses.

After John and Horatio left, I wandered through my unpacked house to my bedroom. I opened my lingerie drawer, pulled out the slightly chewed pink feather boa, wrapped it around my neck.

Back before my marriage crashed and burned, Kevin and I used to dance around our bedroom before we made love. Old standards always, slow and romantic. Diana Krall singing "I've Got You Under My Skin." Eva Cassidy's version of "Cheek to Cheek." Joni Mitchell's "Both Sides Now," not the folky soprano version but the smoky and elegant jazz rendition she'd done decades later on the album of the same name.

These were the CDs Nikki had returned to me via John. They were my finds, the special songs I'd discovered, and I'd left them behind because Kevin had ruined them for me.

I'd once made a life-sized paper doll of Kevin, danced it around the living room, burned it in the fireplace to let him go. And I *had* let him go, so what was it that I was still hanging on to? Love's illusions that Joni Mitchell sang about so beautifully? Or maybe instead of hanging on, I'd let go of too much—my trust, my hopes, my conviction that any future relationship wouldn't ultimately end up in the same awful place.

What nobody ever tells you is that love basically sucks. It makes you ridiculously vulnerable to another person, your heart and your soul right out there, ready to be stomped into smithereens at any moment. And then it happens—you get stomped. So you say never again, and you put all this time into building up your walls out of brick or straw or beach stone or whatever's handy, and then you add a roof.

And just when you're all safe and sound inside, snug as a bug in a rug, some guy comes knocking and wants you to let him in, let him in, by the hair of his chinny-chin-chin. And you're damned if you do, painfully, excruciatingly damned, because really, what are the chances that this time around will turn out to be any different?

But you're also damned if you don't, because now that he's knocking at your door, in all his glory, it's hard to imagine your life without him. So you try to say yes. But your heart and your soul can't stop remembering all the things you don't ever want to have to go through again.

The returned CDs were on the kitchen counter where I'd dumped them. I brought them into the former master bedroom I'd reinvented as an office after Kevin moved out and I'd relocated to the guest room. I found the ancient CD player that was all I had left once Kevin absconded with our stereo equipment.

One after another, I played the poisoned songs as I danced around the room in my pink feather boa, rocking and twirling in my solo slow dance.

I'd loved these songs once. I took them back now. They were too good to be ruined for life. And maybe, just maybe, I was too good to be ruined for life, too.

After I finished dancing, I found my wedding album and a pair of scissors. I sat down on the floor, pulled the first photo from its protective sleeve. I cut Kevin out with a few quick snips.

I went through the rest of the pictures. Me looking in the mirror as my sisters and mother adjusted the baby's breath in my hair. Walking down the aisle on my father's arm. My parents dancing—my mother smiling as my father sang into her ear. Laughing with my friends from college like we'd never been separated. My sister Carol bossing around one of the waiters. Kevin's hand on mine as we cut our sunflower-decorated cake. My brothers and sisters and me all lined up like a sports team for a group photo. My nieces and nephews rocking out on the dance floor, all of them so impossibly young and beautiful.

When I was finished, I had two piles, one of Kevin and one of all the good parts. I thought for a moment about mailing the Kevin snippets off to his replacement wife along with a thank-you note for returning the CDs. Decided I wasn't that petty or silly or mean after all, so I just stuffed them to the bottom of the wastebasket.

I picked up the empty album, ran my finger over the gold raised letters that said Sarah and Kevin and the date. Then I dumped the album into the wastebasket, too.

I reshaped what was left of the photos as best I could, cutting them into circles or ovals or simple flowery shapes. I might never look at them again, but at least I'd salvaged what I could and let go of the rest.

After that I strolled from room to room, not that there were all that many of them in my little ranchburger, flipping my feather boa around as I walked, taking in the outdated bathroom, the trim we'd never gotten around to painting, the hardwood floors that desperately needed a good refinishing.

I carried the CD player out to the living room. Dug through some other old CDs that I hadn't listened to in ages, throwing them into a box as I went so it counted as packing. I found an old classic rock collection CD that I'd won in our family Christmas swap one year. I played "The House of the Rising Sun" at full tinny blast while I sang along at the top of my lungs, using one end of the boa as a microphone.

After the first verse, my microphone turned back into a boa and I picked up my air guitar. My brother Michael had taught me to play this song on his guitar when we were in high school. It was the only song I'd ever learned, but I'd played it over and over again and my fingers still remembered the chords.

"Goodbye, house," I yelled as I hurled my imaginary guitar off the stage. I gave one end of my feather boa another fling. "I hope you have better luck with your next owners."

"What the hell are you doing?" my sister Carol said. She walked past me and turned off the CD player. "And who even listens to CDs anymore?"

"I do," I said. "And I was listening to that one. By the way, nice of you to knock first."

"Put on a front door and I might have something to knock on. And why would you paint your door if you've already sold your house?"

"What are you doing here? I told you I'd drop off your minivan and pick up my car later. I just wanted to get some more packing done first."

Carol looked around my living room. "I can't believe you have to be out of here in a week—I knew you needed help. Okay, I've got exactly one hour before I have to pick up Siobhan at the library. Books first, then clothes, then mementos if we get that far. Where are the boxes? Oh, and by the way, you have paint in your hair."

I pointed in the direction of the boxes. Then I reached for a handful of books. There was no sense arguing with my sister Carol. She was a force.

I heard the water running in my kitchen sink. Carol came back in, managing to hold two flattened boxes under her arm and a carry a half-full bottle of Two Buck Chuck plus two wine glasses at the same time. I looked closer: she was actually holding a small bottle, too."

"What's the nail polish remover for?" I said.

"Your hair. Unless the red paint streaks are supposed to be a fashion statement. Oh, and a bit of advice: Why don't you let John pick out the wine the next time."

She put the wine bottle down on my coffee table, handed me a glass.

"Thanks," I said. "But I think I'm going to stick to seltzer. I've got a lot of packing to do." I reached for one of the boxes.

Her face lit up. "Ohmigod, you're pregnant, aren't you? Come on, tell me the truth."

"I'm not pregnant," I said. "And I don't want to talk about it."

"Fine," Carol said. "Be like that. But don't expect me to tell you anything from now on. And you can get your own paint out of your hair."

Nineteen

Polly and I were gathered with the kids around our circle doing Halloween-themed yoga. We rolled up like pumpkins, stirred our imaginary cauldrons like witches, got down on our hands and knees and turned ourselves into big square haunted houses.

We all stood up again as Polly put the yoga cards away. The second I turned on Michael Jackson's "Thriller," everybody started dancing around the room in what had become our daily game of Halloween freeze dancing. I danced in place next to the CD player so I could hit the pause button and stop the music when the kids were least expecting it.

Some of the more savvy kids moved closer to keep an eye on me. I circled my wrists around while I danced, moving one hand closer and closer to the CD player to fake them out. A couple of the kids froze, re-alized I wasn't really going to push the button, started dancing again.

"No fair," five-year-old Ember said.

"Keep dancing," I said.

They wiggled, they rocked, they jumped up and down. I faked out everybody again by pretending to stop the music and they all laughed.

"Can I paw it?" Juliette said.

In all the years I'd been teaching, it was amazing how many kids used paw as the singular of pause. Or I guess a better way to say it would be they used paw to mean they wanted a single turn to pause the CD player. In a way, especially if you couldn't spell yet, it made perfect sense, and it always reminded me how truly incredible it was that children managed to master our complicated language. It was also so cute that I hated to correct them, so usually I didn't. The way I looked at it was that by the time they were forty they'd all know enough to say pause instead of paw.

I hit the button again. Everybody froze—mid-spin, or mid-clap, or one leg up in the air. I waited long enough to give them a chance to work on their balance. Then I hit the button and the music blasted out once more. The instant they started dancing, I hit the button again, one of my favorite freeze dancing tricks. The kids laughed at unexpectedly having to stop their momentum so soon after getting moving again, and a couple of the three-year-olds toppled right down to the floor.

Polly and I helped the three-year-olds get back on their feet again. Then I led a conga line through the room to "Monster Mash"—around our circle, between the tables, along the perimeter of the classroom, and back to the circle again. We rolled our arms in time to the music, pushed one hand and then the other up over our heads, kicked our legs out to the sides.

Just as the song was winding down, I made my way back to the CD player. I hit the button for a couple of final freezes. After the last notes faded away, we took deep breaths in and reached our arms up over our heads, then blew out the air as we dropped our heads forward and reached for our toes.

"Okay," I whispered. "Now tiptoe quietly over to the door and line up single file. I think it's warm enough to have our snack outside today."

I looked over at Polly, who was already taking a plastic container of cheese cubes and a pitcher of lemon water out of our fridge. We were trying to wean the kids off sugary fruit juices at snack time. The beet juice my father had won during his sweepstakes phase hadn't flown, but so far the lemon water was a hit.

I grabbed a stack of paper cups and a pile of napkins, squished my way in between the door and the front of the line. Zipped my lips, then pressed my arms tightly to my sides. The kids zipped their own lips and pressed their arms to their sides.

Across the room Polly pulled the top off the cheese container. A small army of cheese cubes flew every which way.

Growing up, the kids in my family were strict ob-
servers of the two-minute rule: Anything that fell on
the floor was perfectly safe to eat as long as it reached
your mouth within the next two minutes. This,
however, is not the kind of thing you can get away with
in your classroom, at least not anymore, and it is
definitely not the story you wanted your students
telling their parents around the dinner table.

Some of the kids broke ranks and started running
for the cheese like preschool mice.

"Freeze," I yelled.

They froze.

Tears were streaming down Polly's face.

"Don't cry," five-year-old Millicent said. "It was just
an accident."

"I like dirt," three-year-old Jaden said.

I gave Polly a quick sympathetic look, then opened
the door to the hallway. "Okay, everybody, walk like
this." I lifted my knees high and started marching like
the Pied Piper in the direction of the nearest exit door.

Ethan and June, my former and his current
assistant, were already outside at the picnic tables with
their class.

June and I smiled at each other, and I had a moment
of missing her laid-back spaciness. If June had dropped
something on the floor, she wouldn't have gotten the
least bit frazzled. She would have simply cleaned it up
and then wandered off to meditate.

"Where's your other half?" Ethan asked.

"She'll be out in a minute," I said. "Hey, is Polly okay?" I didn't know exactly what the situation was between the two of them, but it slipped out anyway.

He didn't even bother to dazzle me with his surfer boy smile before he spoke. "You might want to ask her that question," he said. And then he walked away.

Polly's eyes were dry when she came out carrying a big box of Goldfish and the pitcher of lemon water. We got the kids seated around the picnic tables, served them their snack.

We stepped back a short distance from the table. Polly handed me a Dixie cup of Goldfish.

"Thanks," I said. "You okay?"

She nodded. We both stood there, keeping an eye on the kids, popping an occasional Goldfish into our mouths. I noticed that Ethan stayed on the other side of the picnic tables.

"Listen," I said. "Do you want to grab an ice cream after school, or maybe take a walk on the beach or something?"

Polly turned to look at me. "It's okay, Sarah. I'm fine."

I fished another Goldfish from the Dixie cup. "Actually, you'd be doing me a favor. If I go straight home, I'll have to start packing right away. Unless you want to keep me company while I pack?"

"Deal," she said. "As long as you let me help."

. . . . .

I held the door open so Polly could walk in first.

"Cute house," she said.

"Liar," I said.

"Okay, potentially cute."

"Just about any house is potentially cute," I said. "Just like almost any marriage is potentially sustainable."

"Don't get me going on that subject," Polly said.

She followed me into the kitchen.

I opened my fridge wide. John and I had gone grocery shopping together so there was actually food in it and everything. "Well, let's see, I've got cheese."

To her credit, she burst out laughing.

"And I've got wine," I said. "In case you could use a glass right about now."

She shook her head. "No thanks. Water would be great though."

I grabbed two water bottles, handed her one.

She took a long drink. "So, what do you want me to pack first?"

I sighed. "I have no idea. Not only do I detest packing, but I have absolutely no aptitude for it."

"How about if we pull everything out of the cupboards and pile it on the counter. That way we can see what needs to be packed and it'll also look like we're making progress. And the cabinets will be empty."

"Genius," I said. "But given that I have basically no counter space, boxes might have to be involved." I grabbed a flatted box from the pile leaning against one of the lower cabinets, opened it, starting folding over the flaps.

Polly grabbed another box. "So when do you have to be out of here?"

"Next week."

"Wow, that's soon."

"Thanks," I said. We both laughed.

"Did you buy another place? Never mind, it's not my business."

"Not yet. This place is sold and my boyfriend is renting out his condo. And theoretically we're buying a house together if we ever actually manage to find one, but in the meantime we're moving into the house I grew up in. With my father."

"Double wow."

"You can say that again. So if I show up on your doorstep in the middle of the night, just promise you'll let me in, okay?"

"You're both welcome to stay with me if you want," Polly said. "The beach house I'm renting for the winter has an extra bedroom."

"Thank you. I really appreciate the offer, but you'd be sick of me by the end of the first week. It might not seem like it now, but a school year can feel like a really long time." I found the packing tape, cut off a long strip to reinforce the bottom of my box, put the tape and scissors back on the kitchen table. "The truth is I've learned the hard way that it works out a lot better when you and your teaching partner give each other a little bit of space."

"And here I thought you just didn't like me." She said it in a jokey tone, but her eyes filled and her cheeks flushed. She cleared her throat, reached for the packing tape.

"Oh, I'm so sorry," I said. "I'm an idiot. Of course I like you. And I know you don't know anyone around here. Oh, God."

Polly brushed my words away with one hand.

"Listen," I said. "Let's just be friends, okay? But you have to promise me that if you decide you hate my guts before the school year is finished, you won't start one-upping me in front of the kids. Or sabotaging me with the parents."

Polly opened her eyes wide. "Really? Those things have happened to you?"

"If you teach long enough, anything and everything happens to you at one point or another." I shrugged. "It's a lot of hours in a close working relationship. In a way, it's like a kind of marriage."

Polly scrunched her eyes closed. "Oh, no. We are soooo screwed."

"Ha. Sorry for the poor choice of words. It's actually nothing at all like a you-know-what."

Polly pulled out a stack of plates from one of my cabinets. "How about if I pack all but two of these?"

"Perfect. Wait, why don't you just pack them all—we can use paper plates. There's bubble wrap in that box over there."

I opened the drawer that held my motley collection of kitchen utensils. Thought about sorting through and figuring out which to keep and which to donate to charity and which to throw out. Decided that was way too much work and just dumped the whole mess into the box.

"And you're so neat at school," Polly said.

"At the risk of sounding introspective, I might have a slight tendency to be more committed to my class-room than to my life." I pulled open another drawer. "So, what happened at school today anyway? I mean, I know we don't have a big snack budget, but it was only cheese."

Polly didn't say anything.

I looked up, a roll of aluminum foil in my hand.

She opened her mouth, closed it again.

"I'm pregnant," she finally said.

Twenty

"Is Ethan the father?" slipped out of my mouth before I could stop it.

Polly laughed. "No. Of course not. Poor Ethan, he's such a nice guy and he wants to be my knight in shining armor in the worst way—it's just who he *is*. But he's trying to get back together with his girlfriend and, you know, you can't exactly bring your pregnant new friend from school along for the ride. Ethan and I had practically just met when I dumped my pregnancy on him. And now I just did the same thing to you."

"It's okay. I'm glad you told me. So I know it's not my business, but is the father involved at all?"

Polly cut a rectangle of bubble wrap from the roll with one long slide of the scissors. "There is no father."

"Do you mean artificial insemination or immaculate conception?"

She didn't say anything.

"Got it," I said. "You mean none of my business."

She pointed the scissors up in the air and snipped them open and closed a few times. "I mean there is no father. He doesn't know, he'll never know, he wouldn't be the least bit interested even if he did know, and his name will not be on the birth certificate. End of story."

I couldn't seem to stop guessing. "It's your ex-husband, isn't it?"

Polly put the scissors down, took a sip of water, sighed. "I lured him into post-breakup sex, is that what you want to hear? He's got three kids with his first wife, another one with his new wife. I figured the least he could do for his second wife was to save me a trip to the sperm bank. He's got good genes. He's an asshole, but he's got good genes."

"Wow," I said.

"Yeah, well."

"Have you seen an obstetrician yet?"

"Ethan came with me. But no matter what he says, I'm not going to let him go to the next appointment. It's not fair."

"How far along are you?"

Polly turned away from me and sat down. She put her elbows on my kitchen table and buried her face in her hands. "Three-and-a-half months. I hardly puke at all anymore."

I did the math, counting on my fingers twice to be sure.

I waited until she looked up. "You were pregnant when I interviewed you."

She nodded, her head barely moving. "I'd just found out for sure a little while before that. I figured I needed to find a kiddie boot camp of some sort to get myself up to speed pretty fast. I apologize that I won't quite make it through the entire school year, but I plan to work right up until I go into labor, so hopefully I'll make it through most of it."

I just looked at her.

She crossed her arms over her chest. "Sorry I didn't let you in on it. But you have to admit you never would have hired me if I'd told you."

I shook my head. "Legally you can't not hire someone because she's pregnant."

Polly pushed herself up from the table, grabbed another plate off the counter. "Right. And how could you ever have come up with another reason not to hire me when my resumé was so jam-packed with early childhood experience?"

"Good point," I said. The truth was that I had no idea what I would have done, but I sure as hell knew that my bitch of a boss wouldn't have let me hire Polly if she'd known. "Okay, we need to get a plan here. Fast."

"What do you mean?"

"If you're three-and-a-half months pregnant, you're going to be showing soon."

"I think I'm pretty much there." Polly put the bubble-wrapped plate in the box, turned sideways, pulled her baggy sweater tight so I could see the definitive bump of her belly. "So what are you suggesting? A heavy investment in Spanx?"

"No, of course not. But preschool rumors grow like germs in a petri dish if you try to keep the lid on things. Everybody will be whispering and wondering, and there might even be a few high drama parents who don't think you're a good role model for their precious children when they find out you're single. And they will."

Polly rested both hands on her stomach. "You're scaring me."

"Relax," I said. "I know how to do this. We've got to get you out and proud as soon as possible. Like everybody has known you're pregnant all along and how happy we are for you and what a magical opportunity this is for our lucky students to have you in their classroom."

Polly looked at me like she wasn't quite buying it.

"Let me work out the details and then we'll take it from there. Are you okay with me letting some of the other teachers in on this so they can help? If it's going to work, I think I have to."

"I trust you," Polly said. "Do whatever you decide makes sense. And thank you."

"It's going to be fine. And by the way, I forgot to say congratulations." I crossed my tiny kitchen and gave her a hug.

Polly patted my back as if she were practicing for her baby.

. . . . .

John and I were supervising the moving of the pinball machines. My father was nowhere to be found, which meant he either had a hot date or was out driving the Bark & Roll Forever ice cream truck. Or maybe even both at once.

Before the movers arrived, John and I relocated all the furniture in the formal front parlor, always the least-used room of the house I'd grown up in. First we'd rearranged the original dining room chairs, and then we'd moved some of the mismatched chairs we used for extra seating up against the wall.

We put folded beach towels under the feet of an ancient sofa so we could slide it into the dining room. "Are you sure about this?" I said as we shoved the heavy sofa until it was facing one side of the long table. "I still think it might be safer to break down the bunk beds in the boys' bedroom and have the movers put the pinball machines up there. At least there's a lock on the door and we can hide the key."

We tilted the sofa and yanked the towels out one at a time. John made a small adjustment until the sofa was exactly parallel to the dining room table. "They're sturdy machines that were built to be used, and since your dad was kind enough to let us keep them here, I think everybody should get to play pinball. And if they're going to be used, they'll be a lot safer in a big open room with lots of space around them, rather than crammed into a bedroom. Plus, you've already said your nieces and nephews like to use your brothers' bunk beds for sleepovers. I don't want to get in the way of that."

We carried an armchair into the dining room, made a place for it across from the sofa.

I stepped back to get a good look. "This actually looks pretty good. Until the milk starts to spill."

"Maybe we should buy some kind of temporary covers for them?"

I laughed. "Anything that can be spilled on these things has already been spilled on them at least five times. And if you reach underneath them, you'll probably find about eight pounds of ABC gum."

"What's that?"

"Already. Been. Chewed. You didn't do that at your house?"

John shook his head. "It's like I missed an entire childhood."

"Don't worry," I said. "Living here for a little while will make up for it."

Two movers showed up exactly on time, both wearing tuxes and white gloves, John's pinball machines wrapped in puffy white comforters that were substantially nicer than the one on my bed. The movers maneuvered them into the room and arranged them perfectly, turning the front parlor into an instant game room.

"See," John said after they'd given us both white-gloved handshakes and left. "All the pieces are falling into place. Come on, let's get our temporary bedroom set up."

The plan was that John and I would stay in the bedroom I'd shared with my younger sister Christine when we were kids. Carol had hogged a smaller bedroom all to herself, of course, while all three boys had crammed into another bedroom with two sets of bunk beds that had also offered lower bunk guest space for the occasional visitor.

"This is so weird," I said as I took in the matching white twin beds, matching white bedside tables, matching white dressers. Matching hot pink and Kelly green-checked bedspreads completed the look, plus a stray poster of Billy Idol from his "White Wedding" days, his platinum hair sticking straight up, the red background making his black eyeliner pop.

"Which bed was yours?"

I pointed.

John put his hands on my shoulders and steered me toward it, leaned into me until I was on top of the bed and he was on top of me.

"Pretty fancy maneuvering," I said. "Get yourself a tux and some white gloves and I bet you could get a job working with those moving guys.

He kissed me. I kissed him back. He reached for the snap on the waistband of my jeans.

I put my hand on top of his. "Not with Billy watching," I said in my best teen angst voice. "Look, his eyes follow you everywhere."

We both looked up at the poster. "That guy's out of here," John said.

"Actually," I said, "Billy Idol was Christine's heart throb. I was holding out for you."

"Of course you were. But he's still coming off that wall."

"Is this our first decorating conflict?" I leaned back as I said it.

John grabbed me before I fell off my old bed.

"Okay, that's it," I said. "I don't want to spend any more time in this bed until we have to."

He nuzzled my ear. "To be continued."

I rolled up Billy Idol and put him in the closet. John and I moved the bedside tables out of the way so we could push the beds together. We stripped off all the bedding and jammed it into the washing machine. Then I dusted with some old dishtowels and an ancient can of Lemon Pledge I found in the kitchen, while John vacuumed the two matching pink shag area rugs and the hardwood floors and the tiny closet.

"So," John said as he rewound the vacuum cord into a perfectly even coil. "Where is your dad planning to build this man cave of his? I promised him I'd take a look and help him come up with a design strategy."

"He hasn't really said, but it's got to be the secret room." I sat down on my childhood bed, gave it a little bounce. "If you think my old bedroom is hot, wait till you see our high school den of iniquity." I waggled my eyebrows. "If walls could talk . . ."

In one of the many quirks of the old house, the mudroom and the secret room above it were unheated and none of the doors had locks. The only lock at that end of the house was on the door that led to the kitchen, not that my father ever bothered to lock it. John followed me out through the kitchen door, and up stairs so narrow it was almost like climbing a ladder. We stood in the center of the secret room so we wouldn't bump our heads on the ceiling.

"What a great space," John said. "Add a couple of dormers and it would be a terrific man cave. You could even take over the garage below, use some of that space to create a more functional staircase, and you'd have an entire man palace. Then you could build a new garage at a right angle to the old one, or even on the other side of the house."

"My dad's pretty much just looking for a place to put a flat screen and a recliner. And maybe a minibar. It would be crazy to add more space to the house. He only uses a couple of the existing rooms as it is."

"Good point." John ran a hand over one of the rough shiplap walls. "But it's hard not to see the possibilities. This is the kind of house that's worth putting some money into."

I walked along the half wall and unlatched the door to a little storage space tucked under the eaves where we all used to hide our contraband. I pulled the door open, squatted down to peer inside.

I pulled out the pillow first. And then the sleeping bag. And then the candles. Before I even found the iPhone, I was pretty sure I knew who'd stashed it all here.

Twenty-one

I carried the iPhone downstairs with me, pulled my own cell out of my purse, called Siobhan's phone with it.

John was looking over my shoulder as my screen lit up with Siobhan's name.

The other phone rang right away.

"Oh, boy," he said.

"You've got that right," I said. "There's definitely a boy involved. She must have dropped her phone when she was stashing the other stuff."

I ended the call, then tried to access Siobhan's phone. I wasn't quite sure what I was going to do. Delete the evidence of my call so she wouldn't know I was the one who turned the phone over to Carol, assuming I could talk Carol into not ratting me out? Scroll through looking for incriminating texts so I wouldn't feel so bad about turning it over to Carol?

I shrugged. "I can't get in. It's password protected."

"Don't you think you should leave that to Carol and Dennis?" John said. "There's a Polish proverb that comes to mind here: *Not my circus, not my monkeys.*"

"Yeah, I guess," I said. It was a great proverb, but whether it applied to this particular case was debatable. Maybe it wasn't my circus, but my niece was definitely one of my monkeys.

. . . . .

I got to school early the next day and went right to Ethan's classroom. The door was open so I stuck my head inside. Ethan was sitting cross-legged on his classroom meditation chair. The chair was from Bali and it was made out of wood and sat low to the ground, a thick sage-colored cushion covering the seat, a lotus blossom carved on the base. A laminated circle of poster board, a necklace of yarn strung through it to turn it into a pass, hung from a little hook on the adjacent wall. CHILL OUT, it said.

"Good morning," Ethan said. He took a sip from the mug he was holding.

"Good morning," I said. "You know, I was so jealous when I first saw that chair."

"Well, it certainly comes in handy for June."

We smiled at each other, bonding over what it was like to work with an assistant who was absolutely fabulous except that she fell into deep meditation at the drop of a wooden puzzle piece.

"What's up?" Ethan said. Just the way he said it, I could tell that Polly had already filled him in that she'd told me she was pregnant.

I looked around his incredible classroom. Among other things, Ethan had been a set designer before he started teaching. Three-dimensional flowers climbed one wall and reached for a sparkly painted sun beaming down from the ceiling. Styrofoam clouds circled the sun like big puffy pillows. On the far side of the room, black chalkboard paint sliced through the length of two walls and a snippet of ceiling, transforming day to night. Randomly placed stick-on stars actually glowed against the dark paint. The Big Dipper hung from the ceiling. Next to it, a hanging cow jumped over a hanging moon.

I had a sudden random thought that maybe if I ever actually did get pregnant in this lifetime, I could get Ethan to help me decorate the baby's room.

I shook my head to clear the thought away so I didn't jinx myself. "Listen," I said. "I'm just going to cut to the chase. I know you've really been there for Polly, but now that I'm in the loop, I'd like to help. Why don't you let me go with her to the doctor's appointments? Polly said you're trying to get back with your girlfriend, and I can see how . . ."

Ethan shook his head. "If my girlfriend can't handle it, then maybe we're not meant to get back together."

"I'm the reigning queen of self-sabotage. And even I think that's ridiculous."

He shrugged.

"I know a much better way for you to be there for Polly," I said.

"How?"

We heard laughter in the hallway as the other teachers began to arrive.

I spoke quickly. "Your godmother is Polly's boss and you've got her ear. The biggest thing you can do for Polly is to make sure she's supportive, treats Polly well, gives her a chance to come back next year if she wants to."

"Good thinking." Ethan stood up, drained the rest of his coffee. "I'll talk to her today. I know what a bitch she can be, but when I was lost and floundering, she was the only one who was there for me. And I have no problem reminding her of that and asking her to do the same thing for Polly."

I looked at him—his sun-streaked hair, his ridiculously good looks, the way he even managed to make a limp look sexy.

"Ethan Buchanan," I said. "You're a good man."

He smiled his surfer boy smile. "Thanks. You wouldn't mind putting that in writing so I can show it to my girlfriend, would you?"

Lorna and Gloria's classrooms were my next stops. I pulled them off to the side, told them what was up in the fewest words possible, listened to their input. I'd chosen my best teacher friends well, and by the time the first students started hanging their backpacks on the hooks in the hallway, we had a plan.

· · · · ·

I swung by Carol's house on my way home from school.

"Perfect timing," Carol said when I knocked once and let myself in. "I have to drop off Trevor and Ian at separate practices on opposite ends of town, and then I have to pick up Maeve from a play date."

"Fine thanks, how are you?" I said.

She leaned over the stairway so her words would carry upstairs. "Boys! Get down here right this instant or you're both going to be late."

She lowered her voice. "If you wouldn't mind keeping an eye on Her Nibs while I'm gone, it'll save me from having to drag her with me. Pleasant company she's not these days, I'll tell you that."

"Sure," I said.

Trevor and Ian came clomping down the stairs, gave me a quick *hey* as they raced by.

"Later," Carol said. She pulled the door closed behind her.

I climbed the stairs, knocked on Siobhan's door.

"What?" an unrecognizable voice mumbled.

"It's Sarah," I said. "I have something for you."

She didn't say anything.

I knocked again, turned the doorknob.

Siobhan was sitting on her bed, a short turquoise terrycloth bathrobe tied at the waist, her hair wrapped in a white towel, her mile-long teenage legs stretched out in front of her. Tears were streaming down her face. Judging by her puffy eyes and pink nose, she'd been crying at least since she got home from school.

"Oh, Vonny," I said. Vonny had been my special nickname for Siobhan when she was little, and I hardly ever used it anymore.

She let out a long ragged sob.

I sat on the edge of her bed, handed her a tissue. "What's wrong?"

"Everything." She wiped her eyes. They filled with tears again instantly. Saltwater rivulets ran down her cheeks.

I handed her the cellphone.

She powered it on, gave me a quick glance through her tears.

I'd been going back and forth and back and forth about whether to immediately hand over Siobhan's cell phone to Carol, or to talk to Siobhan first. I couldn't let go of the feeling that when Siobhan looked back at this time in her life from the relative safety of early adulthood, I wanted her to remember me as the good cop, the hip aunt who got it, the one who had always been there for her.

I was still wavering when I'd shown up at the house, and Carol rushing out the door had made my decision for me. But as soon as I gave Siobhan the phone, I could practically see the wheels turning in her head as she tried to make up a good story, and I was pretty sure I'd made the wrong call.

I took a deep breath. "So. I found it in the secret room at Grandpa's."

She reached for the charger on her bedside table. "I wonder how it got—"

"Don't even try it," I said. "Your sleeping bag and pillow are out in my car. And the candles."

"Huh?" Siobhan was holding the phone in both hands, her thumbs poised to send a text the instant she got rid of me.

"Siobhan," I said. "I'm not an idiot. I know you and Jeremy have been sneaking up there. "

"Huh?" she said again.

I stared her down.

She blew her nose. "Like you didn't do that when you were my age," she said to her tissue. "Like I don't hear you guys tell all your old stories when you get together."

I took a moment to admire her perfect teenage aim. Then I handed her another tissue. "Come on," I said. "Walk me downstairs so I can get the rest of your stuff out of my trunk."

"But—"

"Now."

Siobhan sniffed, looked around for an escape route. I had a quick flash of her climbing out her window on a rope made of knotted-together sheets if I left the room first, so I turned my back while she pulled on a T-shirt and jeans.

"Aunt Sarah?" she said in a little girl voice.

" I *have* to tell your mom," I said. "Do you want me to tell her first, or do you want to be there when I do it?" We'd been down this path before, and I wasn't sure if it was enough of a choice to keep me in the hip aunt category, but it was the best I could come up with.

Siobhan slipped her feet into a pair of flip-flops, sat back down on the bed. "I don't see why you have to tell her. Especially if I promise you we won't go up in the secret room anymore."

"FYI, you *can't* go up in the secret room anymore. At least not for long. Grandpa's turning it into a man cave."

"You can keep the sleeping bag and the other stuff."

"Gee, thanks," I said. "Like I need more stuff to move. Come on, Siobhan. You know I have to tell your mom."

Her voice went up an octave. "My life is *over*."

"I don't have a choice, honey."

She started to cry again, deep shuddery sobs. "It's like being at Framingham State."

I sat down beside her. "The college?"

"No, the prison."

"Come on, honey. You're *supposed* to be miserable at this point in your life. If you weren't, you'd be one of those people who peak in high school and then their whole life goes downhill after that."

She drew in a long, ragged breath, broke into a new series of sobs.

I sat down beside her, put an arm around her shoulder. "I promise you. Your life is going to get better. Much, much better." I considered the trajectory of my own life so far, hoped I wasn't overselling.

"It's *not* going to get better. It's only going to get worse. So much worse."

I didn't think it was possible to cry any harder, but she found a way to crank it up a notch. I tried to gues-timate how long Carol had been gone. Decided I'd better run out to the car to get the incriminating evidence by myself.

When I got back to Siobhan's bedroom, she was back in her bathrobe with her feet under the covers, still sobbing away.

I handed her another tissue.

"Please," she said through her sobs. "Please help me."

"Damn," I said as her pain found its way into my heart like a heat-seeking missile. "All right, I won't say anything for now, but just don't do it again. And promise me you're being safe."

"Safe," she said between sobs.

I put the candles on her desk, held up the sleeping bag and pillow. "Where do you want me to put these?"

She pointed under her bed.

CHAPTER

Twenty-two

John's short-term executive tenant moved into his condo. John and Horatio moved in with me. To celebrate, we spent the entire weekend packing. And packing. And packing some more.

"So how did Carol take it when you told her about Siobhan?" he asked at one point. "I don't think you ever mentioned it."

"If I don't need to bubble wrap it or cram it into a box," I said, "I don't want to talk about it."

He bounced a tennis ball across the floor for Horatio, grabbed a roll of tape from me, leaned in for a kiss. "Just think about how great it's going to feel when we're finished."

"Don't try to cheer me up," I said. "Packing sucks and I have every right to be miserable."

"Okay, then." Horatio dropped the ball at John's feet and John bounced it again.

I sidled up to him and put my arm around his waist. "Sorry. It's just that every single box I pack reminds me of how disorganized I am. Or how I should be dumping at least half of this crap, but I'm too overwhelmed to figure out which half."

He kissed me again, this time on the top of my nose. "At this point I think the best thing to do is to stop thinking and just pack it all up. We can let everything marinate in the storage unit—"

"Marinate," I said. John was the only person I knew in the whole world who could transform a bunch of cardboard boxes in a storage unit by painting a picture of them *marinating.* I smiled for the first time I could remember all day.

He smiled back. "And then once we find a house, we'll be able to figure out what we need for it. We can take it box-by-box and ask and answer the important question: *Will this bring something of value to our new home or will it merely take up unnecessary space in it?*"

"Awesome," I said. I pulled out one of my desk drawers, held it over an open box, dumped the whole mess in.

John shook his head. "I have a sneaking suspicion that I've just signed on to spend the rest of my life with Pig Pen."

I put my hands on my hips. "Start backpedaling, mister."

"A wonderfully intelligent and beautiful Pig Pen with a great sense of humor. But a Pig Pen nonetheless."

"That's not true. You've seen my classroom. I have the potential to be organized. I just need to be motivated."

"Time will tell," John said.

I grabbed another desk drawer, poured the contents in on top of the contents of the first drawer. "Thank you for helping me, by the way," I said. "I hardly helped you at all with your stuff."

He peered into the box I was packing. "I can't imagine why I didn't let you."

"Thanks."

"I'm kidding. I had it much easier. Most of my stuff was staying. And I would have absolutely trusted you to help me pack, at least under close supervision."

Out of the blue, my eyes teared up.

John tilted his head. "Hey, I'm sorry, I didn't mean to . . ."

I crossed my arms over my chest carefully, shook my head. "It's not what you said. It's just that my breasts are killing me and I'm all crampy. It's probably just PMS. But I can't stop myself from thinking that, you know. I mean, what if? And I don't want to think about it because it's probably not. But I can't make myself stop thinking about not thinking about it."

Hot tears spilled over and ran down my cheeks.

John wiped my tears away with one hand, kissed me where they'd been.

"It's going to be okay," he said.

"I don't want to talk about it," I said. "Please? I can't handle it."

He walked me over to the couch, moved a pile of coats out of the way so we could sit down. Put his arm around my shoulder, pulled me in so my head was resting on his chest, rocked me back and forth.

"I love you," he said. "And—"

"Shh," I said.

His mouth was almost touching my ear. "I have to say this, Sarah. Whatever happens, whether we can have a baby together or not, it's you that I want. However it plays out, we'll make the most of it. But *you're* the one that I want to spend the rest of my life with."

I lifted my head up so I could see him. I tried to sniff and talk at the same time and ended up snorting.

John grinned. "At least I thought I did."

"That was supposed to be I love you," I said.

. . . . .

We were so exhausted from all the packing that John and I considered blowing off Sunday dinner with my family. But we had to drop off some more of my stuff at the house anyway. Horatio was also spending the afternoon making the ice cream truck rounds with my father and we'd said we'd pick him up at my dad's house later. So in the end it seemed easier to go than not to go.

I added my second most comfortable shoes to one of the bags I was taking over there to stash in my old bedroom. "How did I ever end up with so much crap?"

"We're almost there," John said.

"Don't be such a Pollyanna," I said.

We swung by to pick up a pizza and a salad on the way over. John held the big oak front door open and let me walk in first. I stopped at the entrance to the front parlor. Trevor and Ian were hunkered over the pinball machines. Lights were flashing and they were hitting the flipper buttons as intently as if they were the controls on a video game.

I turned to make sure John wasn't about to faint or anything.

"That's great," he said. "It's what they were built for."

I parked two bags on the stairway to bring upstairs later. We headed to the kitchen and added our contribution to the random assortment of pizzas and salads strewn across the kitchen counters.

"I can't believe you moved all the furniture out of the front parlor," Christine said. "And if you got rid of Billy Idol, I swear to God I'll kill you."

"Nice to see you, too," I said. "And relax—he's just taking a little nap."

Christine put her hands on her hips. "Where is he?"

"In the closet," I said.

"He's not coming home with us," Christine's husband Joe said.

My brother Michael reached out to shake John's hand while his wife Phoebe gave me a hug.

"Oh, good," Billy Jr. said. "You're here. We were all hoping to get a chance to talk to you two."

"This better not be some kind of intervention," I said. "Because I am not in the mood."

Eventually we all loaded up our plates and found our seats in the dining room.

"The sofa looks ridiculous in here," Christine said.

"I hope that wasn't your idea of grace," I said.

"Ha-ha," she said.

"Grow up, Chris," I said. "I mean it."

"Rub-a-dub-dub," Johnny said. "Thanks for the grub, amen."

"Yay, God," we all yelled.

"May the saddest day of your future be no worse than the happiest day of your past," Billy Jr. said.

"Sláinte!" we roared. I held up my wine glass with the rest of the adults, faked a sip, put my glass back down on the table.

"Where's Siobhan?" I asked Carol.

"Groundered!" Maeve yelled from the kiddie table.

"Ground-*dead*," her cousin Sydney corrected her.

"Home," Carol said. "It's Dennis's turn to watch her."

I started to ask why he didn't just watch her here, then let it go. Carol looked exhausted—messy hair, big dark circles under her eyes. I probably looked exactly the same right now, so I let that go, too.

We all dug into our pizza as we listened to a series of knock-knock jokes from the kiddie section.

"Knock knock," my niece Annie said.

"Who's there?" the kiddie table yelled.

"Witches," Annie said.

"Witches who?"

"Witches the way to fly home?" Annie yelled.

"Good one," I said. I gave Annie a thumbs up and filed the joke away to use at circle time tomorrow.

The first glass of milk toppled over. The nearest adults jumped up to grab napkins before it dripped onto the sofa."

Billy Jr. wiped his mouth with his napkin, adjusted his button-down sweater, put on his serious look. I loved him, but sometimes I forgot that he wasn't older than our father.

"So," he said. "Sarah and John. Have you given any more thought to buying Dad's house?"

"Actually," I said, "we haven't given it any thought. Basically because we have no intention of buying it. We're just staying here till we find our own house."

"Well," Christine said. "Even if you're just going to stay here, I think there should be rules."

"Chris," Christine's husband Joe said.

"Fine," I said. "Rule number one: get over yourself."

John opened his mouth, closed it again.

"The simplest way," Billy Jr. said, "would be to set it up as an owner-financed sale. You two would make monthly payments to Dad instead of going through a lender, which would save you quite a bit of money in interest. The paperwork could be set up so that if you default on the payments, the home automatically returns to Dad."

"I can't believe you think we'd default on the payments," I said. "Not that it matters since we're not buying the house, but still, it's totally insulting."

Carol stood up, wandered out of the dining room.

"But what if Dad dies?" Christine said. "I mean, if Dad dies, Sarah and John shouldn't get to keep the house if they've only been making monthly payments to him. The house should go back into our inheritance and then they can make an offer on it."

"This is ludicrous," I said. "We're not going to buy the house. But just for the record, if we *were* going to, that would be ridiculously unfair to us."

I took a quick bite of pizza, slid my chair back. "Give me a call when you guys change the subject."

Twenty-three

I found Carol on the front staircase. She was about halfway up, sitting on the step that, after years of childhood trial and error, we'd all discovered was low enough to spy on the floor below but high enough to keep the conversation private.

Over the decades the stairway wall had become a gallery of family photos that gave you a group hug whenever you ascended or descended. My eyes went, as they always did first, to my parents' sepia wedding photo.

My thin, dapper, tuxedoed father had exactly the same smile and twinkle in his eyes on his wedding day as he did now. My mother, in her elaborate lace wedding gown, was looking at my father with pure, undiluted adoration. Her cat's eye glasses had little rhinestones in them that were just flashy enough to make me wonder if I'd ever really known her.

My grandparents' wedding photos were up on the wall, too, as well as my brothers' and sisters'. I'd taken down Kevin's and my wedding picture the day our divorce had become final in a ceremony that involved my father's biggest hammer and the sound of breaking glass while my family cheered me on. There were so many photos that you might not notice the gap unless you knew where to look. Maybe I'd get John to take a selfie with me tonight when we got back to my place. It was about time I filled that empty space.

I grabbed the two bags I'd left on the lower steps, thinking I might as well get them at least halfway up the stairs.

"Where are those going?" Carol said before I had a chance to sit.

"My old room."

She stood up, led the way, took a seat on the edge of the pushed-together beds.

I put the bags on top of my old bureau, sat down beside Carol. "Why so glum, chum?"

She hunched forward, rested her forearms on her thighs, rocked back and forth a few times. "When your worst fear comes true, you've got to wonder whether you somehow made it happen, you know?"

"Cut it out, Carol. You never talk like that."

She rocked some more.

In our family, at least with the adults, you don't put your arm around someone who is flipping out. You give her some space.

She kept rocking. "It's like she went for the one thing that she knew would destroy me."

"Come on," I said. "Tell me."

"It's Siobhan," Carol said. "She's freakin' pregnant."

There are moments in life when your whole world stops like a great big game of freeze tag. I felt that now. And if that's what I was feeling, I could only imagine what Siobhan was feeling. And Carol and Dennis.

"Shit," I said.

"She didn't tell you?"

"Of course not," I said. "I would have told you." I closed my eyes as guilt seeped in. "But what I didn't tell you was that I found her cell phone, plus a sleeping bag and a pillow, up in the secret room. I should have told you, and I'm really sorry I didn't. I think this might be partly my fault." I was pretty sure I'd found the secret room stash too late to change anything, but even for a lapsed Catholic it still felt good to confess.

Carol let out a dismissive puff. "Don't flatter yourself. She would have gotten pregnant with or without you. She's her mother's daughter."

"Don't flatter *your*self," I said. "The fact that it happened to you has nothing to do with Siobhan getting pregnant. She was independently irresponsible."

Carol started to laugh, then she started to cry. I patted her on the back a few times. Then I handed her a tissue. It was beginning to feel like I was spending my entire life handing people tissues. Either Mercury was

in retrograde again or the universe was telling me I
needed to buy Kleenex stock.

"What are you going to do?" I said.

"I *want* to kill her, but I can't because I don't want
to spend the rest of my life in jail."

"How far along is she?"

"She has no idea. Denial is her strong suit, not math.
But three home pregnancy tests don't lie. And to think
she's got an underwear drawer full of untouched
condoms and birth control pills. I mean, I really, really
want to strangle her."

"Do Jeremy's parents know?"

Carol let out another puff of air. "A freakin' pox on
Jeremy's parents. I called his mother. She actually said
that from what she hears around town, the father could
be anyone."

"Ohmigod," I said. "I will take that woman out."

"She also said that Jeremy is quote/unquote *going
steady* with someone from their country club."

"What about a paternity test?" I asked.

Carol stood up, began pacing back and forth. "No
way. They don't deserve a paternity test. They don't
deserve to be anywhere near our family tree."

"Truth," I said.

Carol stopped, put her hands on her hips. "But
before I hung up, I told her that if she repeated our
conversation to a single person, we would sue her for
slander as well as request the court for a paternity
test."

"Good. How's Dennis taking it?"

"He alternates between treating Siobhan like she's ten so he can pretend it isn't happening and threatening to go over and punch Jeremy out. And his father."

Carol threw her soggy tissue in the direction of the wastebasket. It landed on the floor. I picked it up by one corner, dropped it in, handed Carol another tissue.

"So now what?" I said.

"She won't even discuss the possibility of abortion. She wants to have the baby and give it up for adoption. It's my own damn fault—I never should have let her watch *Juno*. It's not that easy in real life. I mean, come on, she can't even give away her old stuffed animals."

"Maybe she can do homeschool for the rest of the school year? You know, sort of like she's just taking an early gap year. I could stop by after work and help out."

Carol shook her head. "Are you kidding me? I think she's looking forward to all the attention she'll get at school. I mean, easy breezy, she has a baby right after junior year and then she still has senior year to hang out with her friends. And who's going to have to take care of her, make sure she's eating well, buy her maternity clothes, take her to doctor appointments? Who's going to end up picking up the pieces when she falls apart? God, I am so angry I can't even stand to be in the same room with her."

"Do you want me to go home with you and talk to her?" I said.

"Whatever." Carol threw another tissue at the wastebasket, missed again.

I'd left the single window open a crack to air out the bedroom before John and I moved in. The tinkle of "Leader of the Pack" found its way up to us as the Bark & Roll Forever ice cream truck crunched over the mussel shell driveway.

"Dessert's here," I said.

. . . . .

I knocked softly on Siobhan's door.

"What."

"It's Sarah."

She didn't say anything.

I turned the doorknob. Siobhan was wearing her turquoise bathrobe and sitting in the exact same position as the last time I'd seen her. I handed her a Dreamsicle.

"Thanks," she said.

"Oh, Vonny," I said as I hugged her.

Tears ran down her cheeks as she tried to unwrap her ice cream.

I took it back, tore off the wrapper. I folded a tissue over and over and wrapped it around the wooden stick as if it was a napkin and she was one of my students. Then I handed it back to her.

When she took a long lap of the Dreamsicle, she looked about six.

"When I asked you if you were being safe," I said, "why did you say yes?"

She shrugged. "I was being sarcastic. Or maybe it was ironic. I always get them mixed up."

"But why *weren't* you safe? I mean, I know you had birth control. Why didn't you use it?"

"I don't know. I guess I didn't want my mom to be right."

I flashed back on the cut-off-your-nose-to-spite-your-face defiance of my own teenage years.

"How's Jeremy handling it?" I said.

"Jeremy is a dick," Siobhan said.

"Welcome to the world," I said. "It has a lot of dicks in it. The trick is to learn to avoid as many of them as you can."

"Now you tell me," Siobhan said.

We both laughed. She rested her head on my shoulder, just for a moment.

She sat up straight again, went back to work on her Dreamsicle. "He already has another girlfriend. This stuck up douche bag from his *country club.*"

I resisted the urge to suggest she might want to work on her word choices, as I remembered how cathartic it felt to drop the occasional f-bomb when my own life was falling apart.

I took a deep breath. "Jeremy's not the only one who can walk away, honey. You can have an abortion. And you shouldn't not have one because your mother wants you to."

"I can't. I mean, I know it's my body and it's my right to choose and all that. But what if my mother had done that to *me*, you know? Or to Maeve, who she always calls her oops child."

"But . . ." I said, hoping the rest of the sentence would come to me.

"I know I'm too young to keep it. So I just have to find someone who really wants a baby. Someone who's old enough that she doesn't want to go out every night, but is still cool enough that the baby will have cute clothes."

"Life is so weird," I said. "You spend this huge chunk of your life hoping you don't get pregnant. And then one day you're finally ready, readier than you ever thought possible. And it turns out to be a lot harder than you thought it would be."

She finished her Dreamsicle, slam-dunked the tissue-wrapped stick into her wastebasket. "Are you and John trying to have a baby?"

"Yeah, we are. But I think I might have waited too long."

"You can have my baby," Siobhan said. "You're exactly what I'm looking for."

"Oh, honey," I said. "Thank you. But we can't do that."

"Why not? That way I'd get to hold it sometimes."

My eyes filled with tears.

"But I mean," Siobhan said, "I get it. If I give you my baby, you'd be the mom, not me."

Twenty-four

In one way it made perfect sense. In another way, it was the kind of thing that, especially if it didn't go so well, could get your whole family a hotel and airfare-included appearance on the *Dr. Phil* show.

As I closed Siobhan's door behind me and walked down the stairs, I imagined taking Carol and Dennis discreetly aside to talk to them. Instead I found Dennis sitting on the couch watching TV with Trevor, Ian, and Maeve. None of them even glanced up when I went by.

Carol was in the kitchen packing four lunches. Her daughter was pregnant and she was packing her a lunch for school tomorrow.

"Hey," I said. "Can you give me a ride back to my place?"

She finished making the lunches, put them in the fridge, grabbed her keys. We rode silently in her minivan through the quiet Marshbury streets.

I waited until she pulled into my driveway, put the minivan into Park.

"So," I said. "Siobhan wants me to adopt her baby."

"*What?*" Carol said.

"Yeah. Apparently I fit the bill both in terms of responsibility level and the capacity for dressing it in cool clothes."

Carol shook her head. "See what I mean? She's seventeen and she's freakin' pregnant, and she's worried about the baby's *wardrobe.*"

"But here's the thing," I said. "I'd have to talk to John first, obviously, but I'd like to do it. Adopt Siobhan's baby. I mean, John and I have been trying, but I have such a feeling that I waited too long. So what if I can't get pregnant, and then I have to watch Siobhan's baby go off to live with perfect strangers? I don't think I could handle that."

"The worst part is," Carol said, "that I keep telling myself I could, but I don't think I could handle it either. But there's no way in hell I'm bringing up another child. I can't do it. I *won't* do it."

"So there you go. I can and I want to. And you can come over and babysit any time you want."

"You couldn't afford my rates," Carol said.

"Ha." I wiped a random tear from one eye.

"This is absolutely bat shit crazy," Carol said. "What happens if you get pregnant?"

I snapped my fingers. "Instant family. And I only have to be pregnant once."

"You'd need to set ground rules for Siobhan, serious ground rules. Well beyond her signing the adoption papers."

"Agreed," I said. "But I still think it could work."

"This isn't just about Siobhan," Carol said. "I mean, what's it going to do to Trevor and Ian and Maeve to watch their big sister go through her whole pregnancy and then have the baby disappear? I mean how will that mess *them* up for life?"

"See," I said. "This way the baby wouldn't have to disappear. It would just turn into a cousin."

My outside light was on, shining down on the Million Dollar Red front door. I could barely make out Carol leaning back against the headrest beside me.

"It's been almost twenty years since I quit," she said, "but I'd give anything for a cigarette right now."

"Ciggibutt," I said. "Remember when we used to call them ciggibutts?"

Carol took a deep breath, blew it out slowly, as if she were smoking.

"What do you think Dennis would say?" I said.

"Dennis just wants the whole thing to go away. It's like he can't even take it in."

"Does Siobhan have an appointment with an OB/GYN yet?"

"Yeah," Carol said. "I found a practice a few towns away, just in case she decided not to, you know, carry it after all, and talked them into giving her the spot a cancellation had just opened up. Actually, the first place I called ended up being that same women's shelter you called. When I realized it, I was tempted to ask if they'd mind sheltering my daughter for the next nine months or so. Or even better, if they'd let me stay instead."

"So how about this," I said. "I take Siobhan to her OB appointments, or John and I do. And also shopping for maternity clothes and anything else she needs."

"You'd do that?"

"Of course. I mean if we're going to adopt the baby, that's how it should work. And I don't know how long we'll be staying at Dad's, but if Siobhan wants to move in there, too, I'm sure he wouldn't mind."

"I don't think it'll come to that," Carol said. "But it's nice to have the option. Okay, let's take this one step at a time. I'll talk to Dennis and Siobhan and get back to you."

"Okay, I'll talk to John."

We gave each other a quick hug and then I climbed out of the minivan. As my sister backed out of my driveway, I looked up at the sky and wished with all my might on the first star I saw that this bat shit crazy idea might actually work out.

. . . . .

I'd left John and his car at my family's house when I took off with Carol to see Siobhan, but I didn't have it in me to climb into my own car and drive over there. So I just sent John a text saying I was back at my place.

"That was fun," he said when he and Horatio showed up about twenty minutes later. "Do you know I think that was the first time I've ever been at your family's house without you? Your nephew Sean is really getting the hang of pinball, and even Sydney—"

He saw my face, stopped. "What's up?"

"Siobhan's pregnant."

"Really?" He looked completely confused, as if he'd walked into the wrong conversation. Or maybe even the wrong house.

I nodded. "And she wants me to adopt her baby. Us to adopt her baby."

His expression didn't change. "*What?*"

"Sit," I said.

Horatio sat. I moved a half-filled box off the couch so John and I had a place to sit, too.

John listened silently while I told him the whole story.

"You do know this is insane, right?" he said when I finished. "So many things could go wrong. To begin with, what if Siobhan changes her mind and wants to keep the baby? Or the boyfriend decides one day that he wants to be a father after all?"

"We'd need to talk to a lawyer who specializes in adoption, of course. Find out how it's done, make sure we've got all the right paperwork signed so that the baby is legally ours. And we'll need to set clear boundaries with Siobhan."

John shook his head back and forth. "Right, and your family is *so* good at respecting boundaries. And I'm fairly certain I've read that the birth mother has to be given time to reconsider after the baby is born before she signs the adoption papers."

"It's a risk," I said. "I'm not denying that. But I think Siobhan will do it. It's the perfect situation for her—the baby gets to stay in her life, but she can still go out at night and she doesn't have to change diapers."

"Diapers," John said.

We sat there for a while, maybe a few minutes, maybe longer. Horatio yawned. My stomach growled, reminding me that I'd only taken about three bites of my dinner. I got up, grabbed the only knife that wasn't packed and a hunk of smoked Gouda from the fridge, sat down again. I sliced off a piece of cheese and held it out to John. He shook his head.

"You've already decided, haven't you?" he finally said.

"You mean," I said, "is Siobhan's baby a nonnegotiable the way Horatio is?"

Horatio's ears perked up at the mention of his name. John and I looked at each other.

A really scary feeling washed over me: If John said no I might just have to do it anyway. It wasn't about loving John less than I wanted a baby. It was more like they were mutually exclusive things. And I wanted them both. What if things fizzled out between John and me, maybe not right away, but a few years down the road, and I had to look back and realize that I let my one chance at a baby slip through my fingers?

"I don't know," I said. "But I don't think I can walk away from it."

He cleared his throat. "What if you—*we*—get pregnant?"

"Then we have two babies and they grow up together. But I just can't shake the feeling that we're never going to get pregnant, and I have to tell you that, for me, doing this would certainly take the pressure off."

John closed his eyes as if he were trying to picture the whole thing, opened them again. I reached out to touch him, pulled my hand back.

"Instead of seeing this as a done deal," he said, "can we take it slowly? Watch how things shape up as they move along?"

I shrugged. "Maybe you can. But for me it's becoming more of a meant-to-be every minute since I talked to Siobhan. I can't help it—it's like I can almost feel this baby in my arms."

Another chunk of silence stretched between us.

"Okay," John said. "I'm in. What's our next step?"

"I kiss you and tell you how much I love you," I said. "And then we stay up as late as we can packing."

We packed and we packed and then we packed some more, quietly, trying to let the enormity of what we'd just decided sink in. We piled the boxes that were going to the storage unit out in the garage, left the ones headed for my father's house near the front door.

It was well after midnight when John took Horatio out for one last pee and we crawled into bed. I fell into a deep, heavy sleep almost immediately.

I dreamed that Siobhan and Polly both moved in with John and me at my father's house. Siobhan was staying in Carol's old room and Polly was sleeping in one of the bunks in the boys' bedroom.

John and my dad went off to play pinball, and in my dream I could hear the bing-bing-bing as they stood side-by-side at the two pinball machines and hit the flipper buttons. Polly and Siobhan and I were sitting in tall-backed upholstered chairs in the front parlor, which somehow hadn't really been turned into a game room after all. Needlepoint was involved, and none of us even thought that was hilarious. We just poked away at the fabric held taut by our embroidery hoops and executed one perfect cross-stitch after another.

It was a soft, muted, sepia dream. I shivered as I realized we were in a scene from *Little Women*. Except that we were all pregnant. The babies we were carrying were all girls and we'd already named them Jo and Meg and Amy. They were going to grow up like sisters, too, which made my dream heart fill up with happiness until it felt like it might fly right out of my chest.

The dream was tinged with sadness around the edges though, that niggling sensation like when you're reading a really good book and you start to get the feeling that something bad is going to happen to someone.

But you don't know yet what or when or to whom.

Twenty-five

The full-day students spent most of the afternoon choosing individual work. Curling up in our reading boat with picture books. Practicing tying and buckling on our big stuffed octopus. Dipping sponge letters into bright orange paint to spell out their names on long rectangular sheets of white paper. Working out simple flashcard addition problems using the plastic abacus I'd saved from my own parochial school years or by counting piles of pennies from our penny tin.

When the kids started to get restless, Polly and I gathered them for a rousing game of Tape the Nose on the Pumpkin. We passed out construction paper noses all around, helped the students who needed it print their names on one side and attach a strip of tape. We taped all the noses to one side of our long tables, ready to go. Then Polly and I carried our big classroom pumpkin and its display pedestal to the center of the circle.

Polly drew Millicent's name out of our Whose Turn Is It Jar, so Millicent went first. As she kicked off her ballet flats and pushed up the sleeves of her pearl-button cardigan, I was reminded, not for the first time, how many of my preschool students were significantly better dressed than I was. We blindfolded Millicent with an orange and black bandanna, which I thought took the edge off her fashion flawlessness, and then we all spun her around and around as we counted.

On three, we let Millicent go. She staggered off in the wrong direction, waving the silver-braceleted hand that held her paper nose back and forth in front of her. Just as I was about to redirect her so she didn't collide with our classroom easel, Gulliver jumped in front of her.

Millicent pinned the nose on Gulliver's chin, yanked off her blindfold. Everybody laughed uproariously, including Polly and me. And as the rest of the kids took their turns, as they taped their pumpkin noses to the wall, the reading boat, the sand and water table, the bulletin board, the pedestal, and the pumpkin stem, it never got any less funny. The thing about preschoolers is that they really know how to laugh.

Polly and I took turns, too, exaggerating how lost we were as we stumbled blindfolded across the room, all the kids jumping in front of us to get us to tape our noses on them. When it was my turn, at the last moment I circled my arm around and around like I was winding up for a pitch and then taped my pumpkin nose to my own nose.

"No fair," the kids yelled.

I pulled off my blindfold, peeled the paper nose from my real nose.

"Okay," I said, "grab your backpacks and line up."

Three construction paper noses had made it to the pumpkin, but I didn't bother to declare a winner, and the kids didn't even notice. The way I looked at it, there was enough winning and losing in the world without me adding to it.

Everybody lined up their backpacks in a single row at the edge of the playground, ran for the swings and the slides and the jungle gym.

I checked my watch.

"Go," Polly said. "We're all set."

Ethan and June had said they'd help Polly keep an eye on our students at dismissal. I looked around the playground until I found them and they each gave me a thumbs up.

It was still hard to walk away but I did it.

. . . . .

That morning, I'd gotten up at the crack of dawn to get some more packing done. I'd wandered out to my backyard with my coffee, trying to shake off my *Little Women* dream. I never would have admitted it to anyone, but even the pink and blue stripes splashed across the sky as the sun rose reminded me of babies.

When I went back inside, John was already working. He was sitting at my kitchen table leaning over his laptop, a cup of coffee beside him. Two slices of store-bought crust-less quiche sat ready to be microwaved.

"Are you sure about this?" he'd said.

I'd nodded.

Now I swung by my house to pick up John first. He came out wearing work pants and a button-down shirt and carrying his laptop. He nudged Horatio back inside and shut the door. The plan was that my father would swing by and pick him up later.

Neither John nor I said anything as we drove. When I pulled into her driveway, Carol's minivan was nowhere to be seen.

"Are you sure you don't want to come, too?" I'd said to Carol on the phone last night. "At least for the first appointment?"

"I can't do it," she said. "If I don't detach now, I won't be able to."

Siobhan was sitting on the front steps, wearing jeans and a cute top covered by an unzipped hoodie, a purse beside her. Even though it was the end of October, she was wearing flip-flops.

John and his laptop relocated to the backseat so Siobhan could sit in the front.

"How was school today?" slipped out of my mouth before I could stop it.

"Don't," she said.

"Sorry," I said.

Siobhan turned on the radio, scrolled through some stations, turned the radio off again. She pulled her iPhone out of her purse, plugged an ear bud into one ear. Jagged pieces of an unrecognizable rap song escaped into the car. John's fingers tapping the keyboard in the backseat almost sounded like part of the song.

When we finally pulled into the packed parking lot of Seaside OB/GYN/Infertility Group, I drove slowly up one row and down the next, looking for a parking space.

Carol's minivan was parked in the last row. I pulled into the spot next to her.

"What's *she* doing here?" Siobhan said. She flung her door open, jumped out, started walking across the parking lot.

I rolled my window down, looked over at Carol.

Her eyes were covered by sunglasses. She shook her head, waved me away.

Siobhan slowed down about halfway across the parking lot so John and I could catch up to her.

. . . . .

I'd almost forgotten why they call them waiting rooms. You can spend hours of your life at a busy OB/GYN practice just waiting. And waiting. And waiting some more.

As Siobhan held her clipboard and filled out her information with the pen that was chained to it, I looked over her shoulder casually just in case she needed any help. Under Reason for Visit, she hesitated and then wrote *Pregnancy* in round letters, adding little curlicues to the tails of the *G* and the *Y*.

Being in a waiting room with my niece was giving me a flashback to the time, not all that long ago, when Siobhan had been bound and determined to get her navel pierced. Ultimately Carol had decided that it wasn't a battle she and Dennis wanted to pick with her. In the scheme of things it was better than either a permanent tattoo or an older boyfriend, or even an out-of-the-country piercing experience during a school trip where who knew what the hygiene standards might be. Carol had even decided that this would be my Christmas present to Siobhan, because that way she could hang on to some vestige of parental disapproval.

Somewhere midstream—maybe it was the poster of a long-torsoed, hard-bodied, bikini-clad woman wearing a sexy navel ring that was hanging across from us on the waiting room wall that did it—I'd morphed from chaperone to co-conspirator when I decided to get my own belly button pierced, too. Siobhan had been so much braver than me, but I'd hung in through the burning pain and waves of nausea, and it had been enough for her to proclaim me the coolest aunt ever.

But as it does with so many things in life, the novelty had worn off. Even though John's first gift to me had been a diamond-studded navel ring, eventually I was simply over the whole pierced belly button thing. In the midst of a high drama fight with him, I'd unscrewed the little ball at the top of it and yanked out his ring.

John and I recovered from the fight, and the navel ring went on to live in my jewelry box. I knew it wasn't anatomically possible, but I had to admit that part of the reason I knew I'd never wear it again was that I had this crazy feeling that if I ever actually did give birth to a baby, it might come out holding it in its tiny fist like a brass ring on a carousel.

As Siobhan returned her clipboard to the reception desk, I looked around the waiting room. A dressed-for-success woman tapped one toe of her nosebleed-high heels as she texted away on her phone. Another woman wearing yoga pants and a pashmina draped over her T-shirt nursed her infant unobtrusively. The woman next to her had a small frame and the biggest belly I'd ever seen, as if she were about to deliver sextuplets any second. A couple about John's and my age looked tense and sad, or maybe I just thought they did.

John was typing away on his laptop, stopping every so often to push his glasses farther up the bridge of his nose. I wondered if he'd been too stressed out to put in his contacts this morning. I tried to imagine looking back on this moment from a comfortable distance and saying to him, *Remember that first appointment? When you decided to work remote, I bet you never expected you'd be doing it* there.

A nurse called Siobhan's name and they went off together. John and I looked at each other. I shrugged.

Siobhan came back a few minutes later and sat down again. She pushed up the sleeve of her hoodie and showed me the Bandaid stretched across the inside of her elbow.

She reached for a copy of *People* and began flipping through. I looked around, started to grab a copy of *Parenting*, hesitated, picked up *Home and Garden* instead. I scrolled through the table of contents, but the words might have been in another language for all the sense they made.

Just when I was starting to think it would never happen, another nurse stepped into the waiting area. She looked down at the clipboard she was holding, called Siobhan's name.

Without glancing at me, Siobhan stood up and walked away holding her *People* magazine, her purse still on the floor. I picked up the purse and put in on my lap, had this crazy urge to start bouncing it up and down on my knees while I sang "Trot Trot to Boston" to it.

John looked up from his laptop. I shrugged again.

Time passed. And then more time passed. I used the restroom while John watched Siobhan's and my purses. When I got back, John took a turn while I babysat his laptop.

At long last the nurse came out again and walked right over to us. "You can come in now," she said.

CHAPTER

Twenty-six

John and I walked into the examining room. Siobhan was lying on her back, a white johnny decorated with tiny yellow flowers pulled up to expose her abdomen, a paper sheet covering her from bikini height down. The first thing I noticed was that she'd stopped wearing her navel ring, too. Maybe we should have given each other friendship bracelets instead, I thought randomly.

"*There* they are," a doctor said to us in one of those sing-songy voices that doctors use when they're trying too hard. Or they have no social skills. Or both.

"You can stand right over there so you can see the screen," the nurse who'd escorted us in said.

Another nurse glanced up from slathering the entire exposed area between Siobhan's johnny and her sheet with copious amounts of clear gel.

The doctor rolled a handheld device around on Siobhan's abdomen.

I watched the black and white gibberish on the screen across from us, trying to make out something that looked even remotely like a baby. Like one of those optical illusions that if you stare at it long enough, you go from seeing a series of scattered dots to seeing a litter of Dalmatians.

"*There's* our little fetal pole," the doctor said in the same sing-songy voice, as if he were talking to a roomful of three-year-olds. "And *here's* our little flutter."

The nurse put her hand on his, pointed to something on the screen.

The doctor moved the ultrasound thing around for what seemed like a really long time.

The screen went dead. The nurse made eye contact with me, looked away. She wiped the gel off Siobhan's belly, pulled the hem of her johnny back down, helped her sit up on the examining table.

"The egg sac's not in your uterus, dear," the doctor said. His voice had changed entirely. It was kind but distant, matter-of-fact.

"It's not an egg sac," Siobhan said. "It's a baby."

Nobody said anything. The nurse put her hand on Siobhan's shoulder.

"Where is it then?" Siobhan said, as if she were just catching up to what the doctor had said.

"It's in one of your Fallopian tubes," he said.

"Can't you just move it to where it's supposed to be?" Siobhan said.

He shook his head. "But fortunately we caught it early so—"

"Is this a trick?" Siobhan said. The nurse patted her shoulder again.

The doctor was already pulling off his gloves. When he spoke to the nurse, it was crisp and businesslike, as if the rest of us weren't even here anymore. "I don't think we need it, but let's send her downstairs for a transvaginal ultrasound first. Then get me fifty milligrams of methotrexate divided into two shots."

"Somebody get my mom," Siobhan yelled.

. . . . .

I'd started to run out to the parking lot for Carol, then realized it would be quicker to call her cell from the examining room. She showed up with the speed of Wonder Woman, kicking butt and taking names.

Carol brushed Siobhan's hair back from her face with one hand as the nurse explained that when an ectopic pregnancy is discovered within the first six weeks and the pregnancy hormones are still low, surgery can often be avoided by giving intramuscular injections of methotrexate, which stops the egg from growing.

"The trick," she said, "is to move quickly before there's any damage to the Fallopian tube."

"What happens to the baby?" Siobhan asked.

The nurse patted Siobhan's back. "Sometimes the cramping and bleeding happen right away, sometimes it's a bit of a waiting game and can take a few weeks."

Siobhan started to cry. I tried not to look as horrified as I felt.

I handed Siobhan's purse to Carol, and Carol and Siobhan went off for the transvaginal ultrasound. John and I went back to sit in the waiting room. When my phone rang, I stepped out into the hallway to take Carol's call.

"The ultrasound technician has to squeeze her in between appointments, so we're going to be here for a while," she said. "Why don't you and John go home?"

I knew I should have been relieved that Carol had taken over, but instead I felt banished and useless, adrift in a sea I didn't want to think about.

"Are you sure?" I said.

"Yeah. And then we'll have to wait around to see the doctor again anyway."

John looked up from his laptop as I walked back into the waiting room.

"Let's go," I said.

. . . . .

It felt like a million years ago that we'd first walked across this parking lot. I was a different person then, younger and less cynical, someone who thought the universe might actually throw me a bone every once in a while, a chance to turn an oops into an opportunity.

Someone who almost dared to hope that I might really end up with a baby after all.

"That poor kid," John said.

At first I thought he was talking about the baby that was in the wrong place, the one that would stop growing at any moment, and a chill ran through me. A wave of guilt followed as I realized that I'd been thinking about my own loss instead of my niece's. I tried to throw off my self-absorption, but it felt heavy, like a bulletproof vest or one of those lead-lined aprons you wear for X-rays.

"I know," I said. "Poor Siobhan."

"I'm sorry," John said. "I know how much this meant to you."

"Thank you," I said. "And please don't tell me that it probably worked out for the best or that everything happens for a reason."

"I had no intention of saying either. I was going to say, 'Well, that freakin' sucked big time.'"

My laugh came out twisted, misshapen. "You were *not* going to say that. You don't talk that way."

He put an arm around my shoulder so lightly I could barely feel it. "Do you want me to drive?"

"No." I stopped walking, fumbled in my purse for my keys, pulled them out. "Yes. I don't know."

He took the keys, clicked my car doors open, held the passenger door for me.

I leaned against him for a second. "Thanks."

I stared out the window at nothing while John drove.

I was still staring when he pulled into my driveway. He put his arm around me again as we walked across my front lawn. He unlocked my door, walked me inside.

"Why don't you get some rest," he said. "I'll swing by your dad's to pick up Horatio and then I'll stop and grab something for dinner. Suggestions?"

"It doesn't matter," I said.

I left my clothes on the floor of my bedroom and pulled the one big baggy sleeping T-shirt I hadn't packed yet over my head. We'd brought the bed frame and headboard to the storage unit over the weekend, along with the bedside tables and lamps, so I turned off the overhead light and walked blindly across the room. I lowered myself to the mattress on the floor, curled up in a ball on my side, pulled the covers up to my chin.

Sometime in the middle of the night, in the midst of my sad, restless dreams, it occurred to me that I was forgetting something. But I didn't have the energy to swim to the surface and try to figure out what it was.

. . . . .

If I didn't have a job, I might have stayed in bed forever. That way I wouldn't have to finish packing. Which meant I wouldn't have to move, only to pack and move again. But mostly, if I didn't have a job, I wouldn't have to get up. And if I didn't get up, I wouldn't have to think.

But I did have a job so my alarm went off, startling me awake. The alarm clock was sitting on the floor next to the mattress, so I reached over and swatted it off. I opened one eye and checked the time, realized I'd slept for almost twelve hours. When I rolled over to face the other direction, the comforter was pulled up over the pillow on John's side of the mattress. I sniffed. Coffee was brewing in the kitchen.

"Wait," I said aloud. I leaned over my side of the mattress, dragged my purse along the floor until I could reach my cellphone.

I powered it on, checked the date: October 31.

I shot out of bed, jogged to the kitchen.

John looked up from cooking an omelet and smiled. "Good morning, Mary Sunshine."

"Where the hell did you put those rabbit ears?"

John tilted his head. "What are you talking about?"

"The rabbit ears. Where are they?"

"In one of the boxes in the storage unit. Why?"

"In the storage unit? What were you *thinking*?"

John shrugged. "I guess I was thinking, even with Billy Idol in the closet, we probably wouldn't be wearing them at your Dad's house."

"It's Halloween," I said. "And I don't have a costume. What kind of preschool teacher forgets it's *Halloween?*"

"Relax," John said. "We'll figure it out."

I wolfed down my breakfast while Horatio and John ate at a more leisurely pace. Took a few quick gulps of the coffee I'd started diluting with extra milk at the same time I'd switched from wine to seltzer.

John took a more dignified sip of his coffee, put his cup down. "What about this? We cut a big hole in one of the empty packing boxes and put the box over your head. We can tape foam peanuts and bubble wrap all over it.

"What would I be?" I said.

"Moving," John said.

"Thanks," I said. "But I'd be knocking kids over all day. And what if one of them needs a hug? You can't hug your students if you're wearing a cardboard box."

"Okay," John said. "Let's keep thinking here."

We both did a quick inventory of my almost-empty kitchen for inspiration.

John looked out through the window over my kitchen sink. "How about this? We tape a whole bunch of fallen leaves all over you and you can go as Mother Nature."

I shook my head. "There's always at least one crunchy teacher who shows up as Mother Nature. Plus, the kids will be yanking the leaves off me all day."

I made a quick circle around my kitchen, did a loop around my office and the guestroom, headed down the hallway. The tiny bathroom was pretty much the only room that wasn't packed up yet.

I opened the medicine cabinet and the little linen closet I hardly ever used.

Inspiration struck.

"*That's* your costume?" John said when I came out with a big canvas teacher bag slung over my shoulder and grabbed my keys from the kitchen counter.

CHAPTER

Twenty-seven

"Sorry I'm late," I said as I opened the door to my classroom to find everybody gathered around Polly.

"Ha," Lorna said. "That's hilarious. But what are you?"

"Late for School," I said.

In my medicine cabinet, I'd found an avocado and clay facial mask that I'd bought ages ago, used once, and then forgotten about. I smeared a thick green layer of it over my face, leaving holes for my eyes and mouth. I'd covered my hair with a shower cap, and then pulled out a few strands and wound them around some pink foam curlers I'd found in the back of the linen closet. I'd been hanging onto those curlers since my sisters' and my Irish step dancing days. We used to roll one another's hair around them to create banana curls be-

fore almost every feis and feile we competed at, so long
ago that the pink curlers practically qualified as
antiques now. I was also wearing a bathrobe that was so
old and ratty I planned to dump it on the way out the
door when John and I moved into my dad's house. My
final accessory was a pair of big stuffed Winnie the
Pooh slippers one of my students had given me as an
end-of-the-year present a few years ago.

"Well done, sweetie," Gloria said.

"Thanks," I said. "But the real trick will be not
showing up for work like this every day from now on. I
have to tell you it's a real time-saver."

I checked out the other costumes. Ethan was Harry
Potter, his surfer boy blond hair flattened out and
sprayed brown, big round glasses, a long robe, flaw-
lessly executed miniature versions of all the Harry
Potter books hanging from a long chain around his
neck.

"Perfect," I said.

Lorna was also wearing a long flowing robe, a
triangle of black makeup dipping onto her forehead,
two horns piercing her hood. "Who are you?" I asked.

"Maleficent," she said. She put her hands on her
hips. "You don't think I look like Angelina Jolie?"

"Of course you do," I said.

"If I'd thought of it earlier," Lorna said, "you and
Gloria could have been Malicious and Malevolent."

"Lovely," I said. "Next year we'll have to plan
ahead."

"And what are you?" I said to Gloria.

She struck a pose. "The Olympic flame." Her Brillo pad-like hair was sticking straight up and sprayed bright yellow. She was wearing a gold turtleneck and gold sandals, and she had shiny gold fabric wrapped tightly around her tall-drink-of-water body.

"Totally hot," I said.

But Polly was the real showstopper. She was wearing Gloria's Little Bo Peep dress from a few Halloweens ago, the fabric beneath the empire waist jutting out to emphasize her baby bump. The dress was hemmed short so that it showed off her white tights and black patent leathers. A stretchy pink headband with a big pink flower on one side looked like an oversize version of one on those baby headbands people can't resist putting on their newborns. She wore a baby bib that said FEED ME, and a massive pacifier hung around her neck on a pink string.

"You make a great baby," I said.

"Thanks," Polly said. Even without the two red circles someone had drawn on her cheeks with red lipstick, she was glowing.

"We tried stuffing the dress with one of the pillows from your reading boat," Lorna said, "but we were afraid it might look like she was only pretending to be pregnant."

"Before I forget, honey," Gloria said. "My old crib is up in my attic, and I've got a car seat up there, too, plus bags and bags of baby clothes and other stuff. You're welcome to all of it."

"Thank you," Polly said. "Are you sure?"

"Absolutely," Gloria said. "I don't even know why they're still up there. Four kids is my limit. I am done, done, done, done."

. . . . .

The Halloween parade always began in the school's entrance courtyard and then circled around the edges of the playground and up to the playing field, where the attending parents would be waiting when we arrived. I knew some of the parents would have already set up the traditional après parade snack—pumpkin mini muffins and apple cider in Dixie cups—on long rectangular tables in the center of the field. Halloween music drifted down to us from the field's outdoor speakers.

Kate Stone led the way as she always did. This year our bitch of a boss was appropriately dressed as a witch in a long black cape and a pointy hat. She had a small fireplace broom hooked over one wrist, and when she turned around to make sure we were still behind her, I saw that she had a big mole that I didn't remember seeing before on the center of her nose. I wondered if it was making her go cross-eyed as she walked. I tried to remember who'd told my brothers and sisters and me that crossing your eyes would make them stick. One of our grandparents? A neighborhood kid?

The Bayberry students were adorable, as always. One little boy was wearing a black feather-covered hat with a big yellow beak on it. He had black feathers glued all over his black T-shirt and sweatpants, and a black feather boa was wrapped around his neck. As he walked, he repeated "Quoth the raven nevermoah," over and over again, like someone had crossed Edgar Allen Poe's raven with a preschool parrot.

A little girl in Ethan and June's class was dressed as a birthday cake. Candles made from glitter-covered toilet paper rolls were attached to the top her head. The rest of the birthday cake kept slipping down over her knees. June, who was dressed as the tooth fairy this year, hiked up the stuffed fabric cake and held onto it so she didn't trip.

One of the boys was having trouble navigating the path from the playground to the playing field. He was dressed all in green, and a big, green felt-covered board stuck out from both sides of his back like wings. When two teachers deftly turned him sideways so he didn't collide with a tree, I got a look at his Red Sox baseball cap and the miniature baseballs glued all over his front. He was the big green monster, Fenway Park's most famous wall.

Juliette from Polly's and my class was a jellyfish. She was wearing a wide-brimmed hat with shiny blue fabric covering it. Long strips of the same fabric, plus strands and strands of curled ribbon in all the shades of the ocean, hung down from the hat, fluttering in the breeze as she walked. She made an adorable jellyfish, the only downside being that she couldn't see a damn thing. I kept my hands on her shoulders and steered her like a small powerboat.

Despite Kate Stone's stern warning letter, there were also a few kids wearing those store-bought

costumes that come with masks, which the kids were
now carrying in their hands so they wouldn't suffocate
or bump into anything. One little boy who came
dressed as a backhoe had already ditched his unwieldy
costume by the side of the path. A little mermaid had
stepped out of her tail and was wearing it like a scarf
around her neck, her bare legs turning pink in the
crisp fall air. But as far as I could tell, nobody had tried
to smuggle in a live pony this year.

The parents began to applaud and cheer as we came
into view. Some were dressed for work and others wore
jeans or workout clothes. Kate Stone circled the parade
slowly around the field so the audience could get a good
look and the kids could wave and call out to their
parents.

About halfway around the field I saw them. Nikki
had managed to get one of Nikki Jr.'s tutus over her
hips and was wearing it along with a tiny silver tiara
bobby-pinned to her hair. Kevin had a kiddie hardhat
that said KEVIN JUNIOR sitting on top of what was
left of his hair, and a piece of string had been added to
a miniature tool belt to extend it enough to tie around
his waist. That they'd named their kids after
themselves and were now pretending to be them might
have just taken narcissism to a whole new level. I
couldn't wait to see Kate Stone take them aside and
read them the riot act for breaking the no-costumes-
for-parents rule.

I'd completely forgotten about my own costume
until I got closer.

Kevin laughed as he took in my green face and pink curlers. "There's the Sarah I remember," he said.

Nikki elbowed him. "Don't forget," she said, "our closing is tomorrow." And then she actually broke into the "Tomorrow" song from Annie as Nikki Jr.'s tiara twinkled in the sunlight.

Once the whole parade had circled the field once, Kate Stone stopped walking. We all yelled "Happy Halloween" along with her, which was the signal for paraders and spectators alike to break ranks. Some of the kids raced straight for the snack table, others ran to their parents. The theme from "Ghostbusters" began playing for the umpteenth time this month, and kids and adults began busting some moves wherever they could find space. It was barely controlled chaos, so the teachers and assistants made the rounds, holding the hands of the kids who needed it, escorting them to the snack line or helping them find their parents.

I spotted Polly surrounded by a circle of kids begging for a chance to try her ginormous pacifier. She was laughing and holding it up over her head so they couldn't reach it. A few yards away, a group of moms with foiled blondish hair were whispering to one another as they checked out Polly, still the mean girls they must have been in middle school. They were all wearing nearly identical exercise wear, and my first thought was that I wouldn't want to run into them in a dark Zumba class.

My second thought was to protect Polly. I took a few steps in her direction, but Lorna beat me to it. She swung by Polly first, put a hand on her shoulder, then grabbed the pacifier and pretended to put it in her own mouth as the kids roared with laughter. Then Lorna walked right up to the mean moms, covered her mouth as she leaned in and whispered to them. A dialog I couldn't make out followed. Lorna gave them a serious look, and the foiled heads bobbed up and down.

Lorna made a loop behind the snack tables, reached between two of the volunteer parents manning the table so she didn't have to stand in line, grabbed a pumpkin mini muffin and popped it into her mouth. Then she worked her way over to me.

"What did you say to them?" I asked.

She brushed some pumpkin muffin crumbs off her Maleficent robe. "That Polly's husband is on a mission for the CIA. And for her own protection she has to pretend she's a single mom. I told them not to say a word to anyone, especially Polly, and they swore up and down they wouldn't. So it'll be all over town before lunchtime."

"Do you think they actually believed you?"

Lorna stretched her arms out to her sides. "Of course they did. I'm Maleficent."

"But why make something up? Polly has every right to be single and pregnant."

"I figured this way they'll throw Polly a shower, just so they can try to get some good CIA stories out of her. I've seen some of the baby presents those moms give. I mean, we're talking Olympic level competitive gifting here."

Kate Stone was moving in our direction. Lorna and I executed kneejerk turns away from each other, like kids who'd been caught talking when they shouldn't be. Our bitch of a boss walked right by us and headed straight for Polly.

It was like that vintage E.F. Hutton commercial when the crowd freezes and everybody listens. Kate Stone said something to Polly. Polly smiled. Kate Stone put her hand on Polly's baby bump, just for a moment, but long enough that anybody who was looking couldn't miss it. When she pulled her hand away, it was almost as if it hadn't happened. Then our bitch of a boss smiled again and walked away.

Polly looked over and caught my eye. We walked casually toward each other, met in the middle.

"Well, that was kind of creepy," Polly said.

"But effective," I said.

Polly nodded in my former husband's direction. Kevin was trying to hang onto his mini yellow construction hat while he attempted to pull Kevin Jr., who was wearing a tie and one of Kevin's suit jackets with the sleeves rolled up, off another little boy. The other boy was dressed as a bag of jellybeans. He was wearing a clear trash bag with holes cut for his arms and legs tied with a bow around his neck and filled with inflated balloons. Kevin Jr. had already popped about a third of them.

My wasband finally got a good grip on his mini me and lifted him off the bag of jellybeans. Kevin Jr., his feet kicking away a mile a minute, grabbed the construction hat off his father's head and threw it like a Frisbee.

"Karma is a boomerang," I said.

"I can't believe you used to be married to that dweeb," Polly said.

Twenty-eight

The mattress was gone when I got home from school, picked up and taken to the Marshbury Transfer and Recycling Center, aka the dump, along with my lumpy couch, some rickety lawn chairs, and a broken lawnmower by the handyman we'd hired to fix all the little things that the buyers' home inspector had found.

The people buying my house were first-time buyers. They'd asked if I'd be willing to include the washer and dryer as well as the refrigerator in the sale of the house, and I'd agreed. These were the same appliances that the people Kevin and I had bought the house from over a decade ago had left for us. I wondered how the new owners would feel when they realized that the refrigerator had long ago given up the ghost when it came to defrosting. And that you had to either lean on the washer or put two king-size jugs of laundry detergent on top of it to get it to fully execute the spin cycle. I wondered if they'd go out and buy new appliances after all, or if they'd just try to overlook the parts that weren't functional, the way that Kevin and I had tried to ignore so many things in our marriage.

John looked up from unscrewing the legs of my kitchen table.

"Hey," I said.

"We're almost there," he said.

Horatio barked belatedly and came running into the kitchen wearing a Halloween costume. His front legs were covered in Superman tights, and tiny stuffed arms dangled from either side of the big S on his chest. An attached red cape stretched across his back, elastic strips looped around his back legs holding it in place.

"I figured we could use a little levity around here," John said.

"This is true," I said. I leaned over and rubbed Horatio's ears. "You both make great Supermen."

John smiled. "While we were out flying around, we picked up some Halloween candy, too."

"Thank you. For everything." I grabbed a box and a garbage bag and carried them into the bathroom. Thought about washing the caked green mask off my face, then momentarily decided that if I kept it on I'd still be in costume, which meant I wouldn't have to get dressed today. My final verdict was that leaving it on would be pretty pathetic, even for me, so I spent the next five minutes or so scrubbing all the green off my face, which might possibly have involved removing several layers of skin.

I had to admit my face was glowing though. I dried it with a paper towel, then I rolled up the ratty bathrobe I was wearing and stuffed it into the garbage bag. I pulled my sleep T-shirt on over the tank top and yoga pants I'd been wearing under my costume so I wouldn't have to change again once we got to my dad's. I couldn't make myself part with my pink foam curlers so I threw them in the box along with the shower cap.

I emptied the medicine cabinet, dumping everything shelf-by-shelf into the box, then piled all the stuff from my tiny linen closet on top of that. I unclipped the plastic shower curtain from the rings, left the rings for the new owners and jammed the sheet of plastic into the garbage bag. Moved the shampoo and conditioner and the bar of soap to the sink until I could find a plastic bag to put them in so I wouldn't have to shop for replacements right away.

Between the trunks and the seats of our two cars, John and I managed to get the kitchen table and chairs and the bathroom stuff and the coffeemaker and the last two mugs moved to the storage unit.

"What about the trick or treaters?" John said as he closed the door to the storage unit again. "Do you think we should hang around at your place long enough to hand out the candy?"

"Nah," I said. "Let's just leave a bowl of candy on the front steps." Which meant we had to swing by the dollar store to buy a bowl since all mine were packed. Before we'd finished cleaning everything that needed it and sweeping the floors, the first trick or treaters were ringing my doorbell.

John swung open the door. "Trick or treat," a little astronaut and a little alien said in unison. A young couple hovering a few feet away on the walkway waved, flashlights in hand, their costumed dog on a leash.

John and I waved back. Horatio came running out, wedged himself between John's feet and started barking away at the other dog.

"What's he?" the little astronaut said.

"Superdog," John said. "How about yours?"

"A hippie," the little alien said.

John held out the bowl of candy. Just as the kids went in for two-fisted grabs, I pulled the bowl back and dropped two pieces each into their plastic pumpkins.

John asked the kids how the trick or treating was going so far. He listened carefully to their answers, fully engaged.

The little alien looked past John and me into the house, ready to walk right in. "You got any kids in there we can play with?" he said.

Twenty-nine

When I pulled into the driveway of the house I'd grown up in, there appeared to be a party going on. My headlights lit up a Granny Smith green Volkswagen convertible with an oversize silk daisy decorating the antenna and a bumblebee-yellow jeep with a bumper sticker that read SEXY SALSA DANCER INSIDE. In front of them I could see the pink ice cream truck parked next to my father's sea green Mini Cooper.

John pulled in beside me, turned off his headlights, lowered his passenger window. I lowered the window on the driver's side.

"Would you rather spend the night at a hotel instead?" John said.

I shook my head. "If it gets bad, we can just make peanut butter sandwiches for dinner and tiptoe up to my room with them."

We remembered to bring Horatio in through the kitchen door so he didn't go ballistic when he crossed the front porch. John unclipped his leash as soon as we got inside, and Horatio took off like he owned the place.

The rich cheesy smell of homemade macaroni and cheese greeted us. I grabbed two plates from the cupboard, handed one to John, scooped a big mound onto my plate. Reached for the dish of steamed broccoli.

We sat at the scratched pine trestle table and chowed down.

"What a ridiculously long day," I said.

"We're here," John said.

"So that explains it," my father said as he walked into the kitchen. "I was wondering how Homer got in here all by himself." My father was wearing a white apron and a tall chef's hat that said KISS THE COOK. One pocket of the apron was filled with candy. Bark & Roll Forever business cards attached to dog treats poked out of the other.

He saluted John with his beer bottle, leaned over so I could kiss him on the cheek.

"Sorry," I said. "We were on our way in to say hello, but we got waylaid by the mac and cheese." I took another quick bite. "*Soooo* good."

My father walked over and swung open the freezer. Covered aluminum trays took up almost every square inch of space. He wiggled his bushy white eyebrows in our direction. "The girls are paying me in casseroles. It took some negotiating, but I finally won them over to my way of thinking. Keeps me from making too much moolah and having to take a hit on my social security. Uncle Sam doesn't need any more handouts from Billy Boy Hurlihy, ain't that the sweet truth."

"Actually," John said, "once you reach full retirement age, you can make as much money as you want without your social security benefits being reduced."

"Sure, that's what they'd like you to believe." My dad took a long slug of beer. "But all I have to say is that if Uncle Sam wants to come after my casseroles, let him try it."

"Just as long as you're not doing it to keep me from attempting to cook while we're staying here," I said.

My dad made a face at John over my head. "Heaven forbid, Sarry girl, heaven forbid."

My plate clean, I headed for the fridge to get some milk. My dad reached past me and grabbed another bottle of beer, opened it on the cabinet pull that doubled as a bottle opener, handed it to John.

I drained the whole glass of milk, standing in the kitchen I'd grown up in, and then I started to put the leftovers away while John loaded the dishwasher.

My father watched for a moment or two, nodding his head as if he were supervising. "Saved by the bell," he said when the doorbell chimed. He patted his treat-filled pockets and moseyed away, while John and I finished cleaning his kitchen.

Horatio didn't even glance up when we joined everybody in the family room. He was in downward dog position, backing away from a litter of wobbly puppies on a mission to catch him.

"Aww," I said. I counted six fluffy black and white puppies, added one more as it broke away from sucking on the toe of one of my father's shoes and joined the chase.

"Hi," I said to the Bark & Roll ladies. "Nice to see you again. I'm Sarah and this is John."

"Just to refresh your memories, kids," my father said. "This is Betty Ann and her friends."

"Doris," one of the other women said.

"Marilyn," the other one said.

John hadn't taken his eyes off the puppies. "What are they?" he asked.

"The mother's some kind of Benji mix," Doris said. "She's got one black eye like a pirate. I'd guess she's a Tibetan terrier mixed with a Catahoula leopard dog."

"Or maybe a labradoodle mixed with a bichon frise and a border collie," Betty Ann said. "Sweet thing."

"And the father's anybody's guess, at least until the pups get a little bit older and start giving some clues," Marilyn said.

"Are you fostering them?" John asked.

Doris shook her head. "No, we're just boarding their mom and them for a few days. The couple that's fostering them for the Marshbury Animal Shelter hopped a plane to spend Halloween with their grandchildren."

"We brought the puppies with us to give their mother a break," Betty Ann said. "Those babies are wearing her out. And also to start getting the pups socialized. So grab a handful of fur balls and help us out."

John and I didn't have to be asked twice. We each managed to pick up two wiggly pups at once and carry them over to the unoccupied loveseat. While I kept one from diving off my lap with one hand, I held the other up to my nose. "Oh, that puppy smell," I said.

John was bouncing his puppies up and down on his knees. "Are they spoken for yet?"

"They sure are," Doris said. "And there's a waiting list a mile long if anybody changes their mind."

A flash of disappointment crossed John's face.

"Mom was the one the shelter was worried about," Marilyn said. "But it looks like it's going to be yet another failed foster."

"What's that?" I said.

"A failed foster," Betty Ann said, "is when the people doing the fostering fall in love with the dog and decide they can't let it go. Once the pups are all adopted, the shelter will have the mom spayed and then she'll be their forever dog."

Horatio let out a little bark as the three puppies still on the floor backed him into a corner. When Horatio leaned forward tentatively, a puppy started sucking on one of the stuffed arms hanging from his Superdog costume. The pups we were holding began wiggling like crazy, so John and I returned them to their brothers and sisters.

My dad stood up. "How about a little game of pinball?" he said to John as if they'd been his pinball machines all along.

"Sure," John said, "but you might have to show me how it's done, Billy."

Horatio was right on their heels. Before the puppies could follow, Betty Ann started scooping them up. She handed two each to Marilyn, Doris and me, then she cradled the runt of the litter in her arms as she sat down again.

None of the three women were wearing the hot pink BARK & ROLL FOREVER T-shirts and black spandex tights with the hot pink racing stripes I'd first seen them in. Instead they were dressed in long flowing gown-like robes, filmy and multi-layered and ethereal, all in rich jeweled shades. Their white Skechers sneakers with the memory foam insoles were gone, too, and instead they were wearing sandals that looked like they had good arch support. Except for the three magic wands on the coffee table, I might not have known they were wearing Halloween costumes.

Shimmering in the lamplight, their hair was long and flowy, too, and it ranged in color from salt and pepper to sterling silver to snow white. Doris was wearing at least one ring on each of her ten fingers. Marilyn had three holes in one ear, each with a little purple stud in it, and a single hoop in her other ear. I could just make out the tattooed block letters on the inside of Betty Ann's wrist: ROCK ON.

I had the oddest feeling that I was back in a chapter of *Little Women* again, sitting around as Jo and Meg and Amy and Beth, but instead of embroidery hoops we were all holding puppies.

"I don't know which one of you made it," I said, "but that macaroni and cheese was out of this world." I started to ask for the recipe as if I might make it myself one day, but wasn't sure I could pull it off with a straight face.

They all burst out laughing.

Betty Ann pulled it together first. "We all gave up cooking years ago."

"For me," Marilyn said, "it was the year my second husband ran off with his yoga instructor." She twisted one of the rings around on her finger. "I mean, come on, dude, show some originality."

"For me," Doris said, "It was after I finished my final round of chemo and food finally started tasting good again. And even better if someone else cooked it."

"One morning I woke up," Betty Ann said, "and decided that, to the best of my ability, I was going to live the life that gave me pleasure. Cooking just never really did it for me."

"I peaked in 1969," Marilyn said, "with the Crown Roast of Frankfurters from the Weight Watchers recipe cards."

"I made that, too," Betty Ann said. "In fact, I still have mine. I just gave it a couple coats of boat varnish so it would last forever."

"I remember that the hot dogs stuck straight up in a circle like a crown," Doris said. "But what was it stuffed with again?"

"Cabbage and poppy seeds and pimento," Marilyn said. "I mean, really, what else?"

"I remember my mother had a red box filled with Betty Crocker recipe cards," I said. "They're probably still somewhere in the kitchen."

"Bologna Biscuits with Vegetables," Doris said.

"Oven Porcupines," Marilyn said. "And let's not forget the Campside Quickie."

"It's been a while," Betty Ann said, and we all laughed.

Marilyn counted the ingredients off on her fingers. "A can of French-style green beans, a can of condensed cream of mushroom soup, a couple of cans of chicken, and a package of chow mein noodles. You just fire it up on the camp stove, pour glasses of Tang all around, and voilà, breakfast."

"I'm not sure where the recipe came from," I said, "but on hot summer days my mother would add shrimp and peas and all this other stuff to a fish mold and then pour clear gelatin over it and stick it in the refrigerator. By the time she put it on the table, it looked like all this disgusting stuff was swimming around in the fish's jiggly stomach." I shivered at the memory. "Eventually we hid the recipe on her, but I always gave that one credit for my lack of interest in cooking."

"It's a different world now," Doris said. "You can get through your whole life without cooking."

Betty Ann held up the runt of the litter, gave its fluffy head a kiss. "So long story short, we pay your dad in casseroles we get from a friend who not only loves to cook but runs a catering business. Actually it's a barter—when she's got a big gig, we watch her two dogs for her so they don't eat the profits."

"You might not want to mention it to your dad though," Doris said. "I think he has a little fantasy going about Betty Ann slaving over a hot stove for him."

Their laughter filled the room like music.

"That's my dad," I said.

While I sat there cuddling the two puppies, the whole bark & roll forever thing hit me like an epiphany, and I found myself hanging on to every word these rebel goddesses said. They were ageless and vibrant, and I wished my mother had lived long enough to get to hang out with them, because she would have fit right in.

I couldn't wait to be like them myself one day, as if after all these years I finally had some incentive to actually grow up. I wanted to bark & roll forever, too.

CHAPTER

Thirty

After the Bark & Roll Forever ladies and the puppies left, John and I brought Horatio's and our stuff in from our cars. Then John took Horatio out for a final pee.

"Homer and I think we're going to call it a night," my father said when John and Horatio came back inside. He picked up Horatio's monogrammed dog bed and headed for the stairs, Horatio hot on his heels.

"Are you okay with that?" I asked John.

He shrugged. "Homer, I mean *Horatio*, knows where to find me."

John and I were right behind them, carrying our pillows and my comforter. We stretched a king size sheet over both mattresses of the pushed-together twin beds in Christine's and my old room, added a flat sheet.

I set the alarm on my phone, and we climbed in and conked out almost immediately.

I'd thought Horatio would show up sometime in the middle of the night. But when I woke up just before my alarm went off, John and I were alone in the room and John was snoring.

My old mattress had definitely seen better days. I slid out of bed and stretched my stiff back, then tiptoed downstairs. I put on a pot of coffee and ate some cold leftover mac and cheese while the coffee brewed. I diluted a cup to half-strength with milk, took a sip.

I was just about to sit down at the scarred pine trestle table again when I heard a howl at the kitchen's single French door. I moved the threadbare lace curtain aside and peeked out.

A calico cat looked right at me and let out a loud, pitiful meow.

I opened the door a crack. The cat looked ready to run at any moment, but held its ground.

"Good morning," I said. "Can I help you?"

The cat let out a heartbreaking howl. It was a young, beautiful cat with intense green eyes and white, white fur that looked like it was covered with a sprinkling of beach pebbles in shades of black and brown and orange.

"Are you hungry?" I asked.

When the cat meowed, it sounded like the feline equivalent of *duh*.

"Okay, give me a minute." I left the door open while I scoured the pantry for something cat friendly. I opened a can of tuna with the old hand-crank can opener that had been screwed into the wall as far back as I could remember. Grabbed a fork from the silverware drawer and flaked about a quarter of the can into a cereal bowl.

I put the bowl down on the old brick patio a few feet away from the door. The cat stayed where it was until I stepped back inside the kitchen. Then it practically inhaled the food.

It looked right through the door at me and meowed again.

"Oh, honey," I said. I grabbed the fork and the can of tuna, opened the door.

I was planning to transfer the tuna to the bowl, but the cat let out such a woeful howl that I just put the can down on the patio. I took a step back, leaned against the door.

The cat looked at me, stayed where it was.

"Sorry," I said. I went back inside and watched through the small panes of glass in the kitchen door as it chowed down every last bit of tuna.

It meowed again, loudly, insistently.

"Seriously?" I said. I looked around the kitchen, wondered how it would feel about one of my father's Slim Jims. Grabbed a can of Horatio's organic, ancestral, free-range, grain-free, lah-di-dah dog food and opened it with the pull ring. Filled a bowl with water and put the dog food and the water out on the patio.

The cat devoured the entire can of dog food. It lingered over the water, sipping daintily but steadily.

Then it groomed itself on the edge of the patio, keeping an eye on me through the glass door.

As soon as the cat turned and walked away, I missed it with an intensity that made absolutely no sense at all.

. . . . .

For a preschool teacher, the first week of school can be challenging. The winter months, when the kids have been cooped up inside for way too long but it's so cold that taking them out for even a quick run around the playground might mean frostbite, can also be pretty tough.

But there is no school day worse than the day after Halloween.

The kids stumbled in, bleary-eyed, with matted hair and leftover traces of yesterday's makeup. Judging by the chocolate residue in the corners of their mouths, more than a few of them had managed to get their hands on candy bars for breakfast.

Depp headed right over to the reading boat and fell asleep as soon as he hit the pillows.

"Low expectations," I whispered to Polly. "If nobody gets hurt, throws up, or goes completely hysterical, it'll be a good day."

Polly nodded. The horizontal stripes of the stretchy jersey dress she was wearing made the swell of her belly undeniable. I wondered if it would get harder or easier for me to watch her pregnancy progress from such a close-up vantage point. I tried not to do the sad math. How much younger Siobhan's baby would have been than Polly's. How many months John and I would have been trying to get pregnant by the time Polly's baby was born.

I tried to dial down my wallowing. But I was so exhausted that I decided I needed to cut myself some slack, too. I just had to survive the day.

· · · · ·

As if getting through the day after Halloween wasn't tough enough, the closing on my house took place that afternoon at the bank that was giving the buyers a mortgage to buy it. This being small-town Marshbury, it was also the bank where I was paying off my own mortgage.

John and I sat at one side of the conference table. The couple buying my house, whose names I wasn't even attempting to retain, sat directly across from us. It was like a revolving door was kicking me to the curb at the exact same moment it was pulling them in to take my place.

The couple sat close together, looking young and scared while we signed each paper in the endless pile. As I added my solo signature to their dual signatures, John turned his head and smiled at me a few times, perhaps in solidarity, perhaps keeping an eye on me so I didn't do anything foolish like cut and run midstream.

Nikki sat at the head of the table, funneling papers in both directions. Occasionally she reached for a piece of leftover Halloween candy from the bowl she'd picked up from my front steps during this morning's walk-through with the buyers.

A bored looking suit-clad guy from the bank sat to Nikki's right. A check for the balance of my mortgage would go to the bank. Nikki's commission would come out of the total sale price, and whatever was left would be direct-deposited into my bank account. The buyers wrote a check to reimburse me for two months of property taxes and half a tank of heating oil. They signed over thirty years of their lives to buy my stupid ranchburger.

"So," the male half of the couple said. "You teach at Bayberry Preschool."

"Who told you that?" I said. I mean, the last thing I needed was somebody knocking on my classroom door when they couldn't get the refrigerator to defrost.

Nikki laughed. "Sarah's so popular we couldn't even get the twins into her class."

"Actually . . ." I said.

John gave my foot a nudge with his.

"We're definitely leaning toward Bayberry," the female buyer said. She rested one hand on her abdomen. "We hear the smart thing to do is to call from the delivery room to get on the waiting list." Her other half nodded his agreement, put his hand on top of hers.

Great. Even my dated, inadequate house was going to get a baby. When Nikki handed me another paper, it took every ounce of self-control I had not to rip it into a gazillion pieces and throw it up in the air like confetti.

"It's a great little preschool," Nikki said. "Just watch out for that principal. She called Big Kevin and me into her office and yelled at us just for wearing Halloween costumes. I mean, so what if we like to have a little fun."

In my family, we can say anything we want about one another to their faces, and though technically we're not supposed to, we can even talk to the rest of the family about everybody else behind their backs. But if an outsider tries it, look out.

I didn't want to hear any trash talking about my bitch of a boss either.

I leaned over the table in Nikki's direction. "She's a good principal. And it's not like a notice didn't go home. Just follow the rules and you and *Big Kevin* will be all set."

John gave my foot another nudge, a little harder this time. Nikki rolled her eyes. The guy from the bank glanced at his watch.

I looked right at Nikki. "Oh, that's right. I forgot about you and rules." When I swiveled my head to look at the buyers, I had this odd feeling that my head might keep spinning around and around and around. "Did Nikki tell you that she—"

"So," John said. "How about those trick or treaters last night?" He put his hand on mine, aimed the pen I was holding in the direction of the next signature line.

The guy from the bank held up the bowl from my front steps. "Candy?"

Nikki reached for a Junior Mint. She unwrapped it, popped it into her mouth, smiled at me.

The male half of the buying couple cleared his throat. "About that front door. It's a little bit loud for our taste, and well, we much preferred the original color, which was the color of the door when we made our offer. And so we were thinking it's only fair that—"

"It's called Million Dollar Red," John said. "Great feng shui."

"Fine," I said. "Don't buy my house. I'll keep it."

Nikki laughed like I was joking, turned to the buyers. "Live with it for a little while. If you still don't like it, I'll take care of it."

Somehow we got to the end of the relentless pile of paper, and I found myself holding a blue folder that stated I was no longer a homeowner. As I turned over my keys to the new owners, I started to mention that they might want to consider changing the locks sooner rather than later, since pretty much everybody I knew either had a key or knew where I hid my spare.

But for once in my life I decided to keep my mouth shut.

Thirty-one

"I simply won't take no for an answer," I heard Nikki say behind us when we were out on the sidewalk. "You *have* to let me take you out to celebrate."

John stopped walking, turned around. I turned around, too. Opened my mouth to tell the buyers and Nikki to have a nice celebration, even a nice life. I could be gracious like that when I focused.

Across the street, the new owners climbed into an SUV that might have been bigger than the house they'd just purchased. The doors slammed. They waved.

I looked at Nikki.

She gave me a big smile. "It's the least I can do."

On the one hand, truer words were never spoken. On the other hand, I was pretty sure I'd rather hang from my toes over a bonfire on the beach in August roasting like a marshmallow than spend one more fraction of a second in the company of my wasband's replacement wife.

John gave a little shrug, clearly signaling me let's just do it fast and get it over with.

Nikki sensed her advantage, walked past us and continued along the sidewalk. "We won't even have to drive. We'll just stroll right down the street to High Tide."

John put his arm around me, circled us around like a sailboat coming about, propelled us after Nikki. I tried to picture the menu at High Tide, hoped the most expensive thing on it was really expensive.

My former husband was actually in the bar when we got there.

"Are you kidding me?" I said as Nikki wiggled through the crowd to give him a big obnoxious kiss.

"Forty-five minutes," John said. "An hour tops."

I took out my phone, squinted at it so I'd know what time we could leave. When I looked up, Nikki had commandeered a tall bar table and Kevin was sliding bar stools through the crowd.

"So," Kevin said once the four of us were seated girl-boy-girl-boy around a tabletop roughly the size of a pancake. "Since they don't take reservations, I got here early to get us on the waiting list for a table, but I'd say we've still got another hour or so to go."

"We can't stay," I said.

"Perfect," Nikki said. "We'll eat in the bar."

A waitress managed to work her way over to us, disappeared again to track down some menus when Nikki informed her we were planning to eat right here.

"What can I get you?" she asked me as she handed out the menus.

Since *out of here* didn't seem like something she'd actually be able to accomplish, I said, "Seltzer, please."

"Ooh," Nikki said. "Are we trying to get *pregnant?*"

"Actually," I said, "we're trying to maintain our self-control." *So we don't hurt anyone,* I was too polite to add.

Nikki and John ordered seltzers, too, and Kevin ordered a beer.

Kevin turned to me. "So you finally unloaded the house, huh?"

"I think it was all that sexy lingerie that sold it," Nikki said. "You should see the collection Sarah has, honey." She giggled. "Oh, wait, you already did."

It was all I could do not to lean forward and conk my head on the table.

"I have to tell you," Kevin said, "if I'd thought you'd ever get that much for it, I never would have let you buy me out on the cheap."

"I think you made out just fine," I said, "especially given the size of the commission that's about to land in your bank account."

"Exactly," Kevin said. "I was just going to say that. Things have a way of working out, don't they?"

I opened my menu, held it in front of my face to make my wasband and his wife disappear.

The waitress came back with our drinks.

John held up his glass. "To new beginnings."

"To your next house," Nikki said.

We all clanked glasses.

"A couple of new listings just came on the market," Nikki said. "I think we should get out there bright and early tomorrow morning. You know what they say about the early bird."

I groaned.

"I think we're going to take the weekend off," John said. "We're both pretty beat."

"Okay then," Nikki said. "Call me when you're ready. Or I'll call you first thing Monday morning."

We all turned to our menus. I decided to read every word, hoping that it might turn into a story with a secret portal that I could disappear into.

"So," Nikki said. "I bet you're wondering why I'm drinking seltzer!"

"And I bet you're wondering why I'm drinking beer!" Kevin said.

"Oh you," Nikki said. She leaned over and gave him a big kiss on the lips.

"He's just as excited as I am," she said when she came up for air. "We're pregnant!"

"Congratulations," John said.

"Yeah," I said. I searched for something to make me feel better. "Wow, aren't you two going to have your hands full."

Kevin took a long swig of beer.

"Well, you know," Nikki said. "Three kids *is* the new two."

The waitress, who was probably pregnant, too, the way my life was going, came back. We placed our dinner orders. Kevin ordered another beer.

Nikki started telling John about the houses that had just come on the market. She reached into her bag, where she just happened to have printouts of the listings. I tuned them out, wished I'd hung on to my menu so I could read it again.

"Three kids," Kevin said softly beside me. "I don't know how we're going to do it. The twins are out of control."

"Ya think?" I said.

Kevin took another sip of beer. "We've tried everything."

"That's bullshit, Kevin. You're like those parents I used to come home from work and whine about to you."

Kevin grinned. "That stuff always kind of went in one ear and out the other."

I grinned back. "And that's why you are where you are."

"So what do we do?"

"Give them clear, consistent rules with clear, consistent consequences," I said. "Not a lot of rules, but they need to know that breaking one always means the same thing, like getting sent to the time-out chair, not that sometimes it does and sometimes it doesn't. And make a big deal about it when you catch them doing something right. Kids crave attention any way they can get it, and you want to make sure they're getting it for the positive things. And you might want to knock it off with the junior stuff and always referring to them as *the twins,* give them a chance to carve out separate identities."

Kevin shook his head. "Wow, their teacher said almost exactly the same thing."

"What a coincidence," I said. "And you need to get on it. Once you have a new baby in the house, your older kids will be pushing limits all over the place."

"Three kids." Kevin shook his head some more. "Did you ever think I'd end up with three kids?"

"I don't know. I can barely even remember being married to you. I think they call it selective amnesia."

"We had some good times," my ex-husband said.

"I'll take your word for it," I said.

Kevin nodded at John and Nikki, who were still poring over the printouts. "So I hear that new guy of yours is crazy about you. Even Nikki noticed it, and she doesn't notice all that much if it's not about her. She said all he talks about is Sarah this and Sarah that. And that she's never seen a man so in love."

As if he felt me looking at him, John glanced up and smiled at me.

I smiled back. My heart did that little flip flop thing.

"He's a great guy," I said.

"Then don't screw it up," my wasband said. He took a long slug of beer, put his glass back down on the tiny table. "As I remember, you do have that tendency."

Thirty-two

The tires of John's Acura crunched over the mussel shell driveway. We pulled in behind my Civic, which was parked beside my father's Mini Cooper.

"Thanks for getting me through all that," I said. "Have I told you lately that I love you?"

He put the car into Park, leaned over. We kissed, long and leisurely, as if we were swimming toward each other in the moonlight, with the beach to ourselves and all the time in the world, and not a single bit of packing or moving or cleaning still ahead of us.

We held hands as we walked up the front steps and across the porch that we both loved, stars twinkling over our heads like they were sending us good vibes. John opened the massive unlocked front door and stepped back so I could walk through first.

We found my dad and Horatio curled up together on the sofa in the family room watching a movie. Horatio's ears perked up and he wagged his tail when he saw us, but neither of them bothered to get up.

I held out a check to my father. I hardly ever wrote checks anymore, but I'd turned on the interior light and written out this one in John's car on the way over.

My father raked back the clump of thick white hair that was always falling into his eyes. "And what's this piece of parchment, pray tell?"

"It's the money you gave me to buy out Kevin."

He took the check from me, looked it over carefully.

"Just don't try to cash it yet," I said.

My father held the check up to light coming from the lamp beside him. "Is my very own daughter offering me a rubber check?"

"No, of course not. I'll let you know as soon as the money from the sale shows up in my account."

He yawned and handed the check back to me. "Just put that toward my man cavern, kiddos."

Leave it to my father to manage to make himself look good by refusing the money, and to also wiggle out of the work by trying to put John and me in charge of his man cave. All in one fell swoop.

My dad picked up a folder from the coffee table. "It just so happens I've got a few ideas for you right here."

John reached for the folder, sat down on the couch on the other side of Horatio. My phone rang. I fished it out of my purse, saw Carol's name on the screen, headed in the direction of the kitchen.

"What's up?" I said.

"What's up? What's *up?* Why the hell didn't you tell me you were closing on your house today?"

"Um," I said. "I guess because you didn't ask. Why?"

"Why? *Why?* I had some time to kill between meeting with a client and picking up Trevor from something. So good sister that I am, I swung by your place to see if you needed any help. There weren't any cars in the driveway, so I just let myself in. Clearly John must have been helping you, because it looked pretty empty, but I went room to room, opening closets and cabinets to make sure everything was out of there. I was just about to head out to the garage to see if I could find a broom when the new owners walked in and found me."

"Oops," I said. "And by the way, we swept before we left."

"Yeah, oops. Anyway, they totally freaked out. I think if you and I didn't look so much alike, they would have called the police on me. I gave them my key on the way out, and I also told them that there are probably at least a half dozen more keys floating around town, so they might want to call a locksmith fast. You know, you could have at least left them a flag that said NEW OWNERS as a housewarming gift."

"Why didn't I think of that," I said. "Anyway, sorry. And sorry I haven't called you yet about Siobhan. How's she doing?"

Carol sighed. "She started cramping and bleeding almost right away after they gave her the methotrexate, so that's good. And the second ultrasound confirmed that there's no damage to the fallopian tube. She didn't have any risk factors at all for an ectopic pregnancy, so hopefully it was just a fluke and it won't ever happen to her again. I mean *way, way* down the road. Anyway, they'll check her blood levels next week so we'll know more then."

"I'm glad she's okay," I said.

Silence stretched between my older sister and me, something that almost never happened.

"If you and John get stuck," Carol said. "I mean really, really, really stuck, I'd consider being a gestational surrogate for you. After all, I do have a proven uterus. Obviously, we're talking in vitro fertilization here, not any kind of kinky stuff."

"You'd do that?" I said.

"Yeah. Of course."

"Thank you." My eyes teared up. "Mom would be so proud of you. She always loved it when we had each other's backs."

Carol sniffed. "She'd be proud of you, too."

I reached for a paper napkin from the clay napkin holder shaped like a cow that had been sitting on our kitchen counter since one of us had made it in high school art class, so long ago that all six of us could clearly remember being the one who made it. I wiped my cheeks, dabbed my eyes.

"But," Carol said. "Christine has a proven uterus, too. And she's four-and-a-half years younger than me. She also has one less kid than I do, not to mention substantially fewer stretch marks. So if push comes to shove, I think we're going to have to rule Chris out first."

"I am way too tired to have this conversation," I said. "Good night. Love you."

"Love you, too," my sister said as I hung up.

As if it had been waiting for me to get off the phone, the cat let out a loud meow from the other side of the kitchen door. I grabbed a can of tuna, relieved that my father had either stocked up on tuna or won a case of it back in his sweepstakes phase.

This time I flaked the whole can into a cereal bowl.

I flipped on the outside light so I could see the patio, opened the door. The cat stayed at the edge of the shadows.

"Hi sweetie," I said.

When the cat meowed, it went straight to my heart.

I put the cereal bowl down. By the time I was back inside the kitchen and peeking through the curtain, the bowl was empty.

I opened a can of Horatio's food, filled another bowl with water, traded them for the empty bowl. Then I stepped back and leaned against the house.

The calico cat watched me for a long moment. It inched forward and chowed down. It waited until it had finished eating before it drank anything, just like I always did. It lapped the bowl of water slowly and steadily. Then it sat down and groomed itself.

It let out another pitiful meow.

"Really?" I said. "You're *still* hungry? Okay, be right back."

I opened the cupboard, ruled out a tin of salted peanuts and a packet of instant oatmeal. Grabbed one of my father's Slim Jims and peeled off the wrapper.

"Sorry," I said as I stepped out on the patio again. "I'll try to get to the grocery store tomorrow for cat food. Do you have a brand preference?"

The cat meowed, long and loud.

"Okay," I said. "I'll look for it. Here, try this to tide you over. If it's not your thing, I'll open another can of tuna for you."

I put the Slim Jim down on the patio, walked backwards until my back touched the house.

The cat approached the Slim Jim cautiously, sniffed it, picked it up.

It carried the Slim Jim in its tiny mouth like a dog with a bone and disappeared into the darkness.

"Goodnight," I called to the calico cat. "Sleep tight."

. . . . .

As soon as I slid in next to John, I realized that sitting down had been a big mistake. I was so tired I might not ever be able to stand up again.

"Check this out," John said. He nodded at a sketch he'd made on the front of my father's folder.

I tried to focus on it, but my brain felt like it was packed in cotton balls.

My father pointed. "See, that's where the old garage used to be, and those are the new stairs. And look at all that head room those bumpout thingamajiggers give me."

I shot John a look. "Dad, the last thing you need is more space in this house."

"That's my point entirely," my father said. "All's I want is my man cavern. You and your young man can have the rest of it. Homer can set his own schedule and divide his time between us. It's the perfect solution—all four of us will be in fat city."

"What?" I said. "*What?*"

"We'll have no wiggin' out on my watch, young lady," my father said. "You look like you're ready to start eatin' the grapes right off the wallpaper."

"Thanks," I said.

I swiveled my head in John's direction. "When did *this* happen?" I could feel a fight coming on. One of those great big high drama fights that you either survive or look back on as the one that was the beginning of the end. I mean, whose father was this anyway?

John shrugged. "Nothing has happened. It's just an interesting idea, that's all."

"Take her through it, Johno," my father said.

"Yeah," I said. "Take me through it, Johno."

I tried to relax my shoulders, but they seemed to have worked their way up around my ears.

"Well," John said. "An architect would need to be brought in, obviously. But one way it could work would be to make the kitchen and this family room and the front parlor with the pinball machines a shared space—"

"As long as I have a minibar and a microwave in my man cavern to go along with that 72-two incher and the recliner with dual beverage holders you kids are going to spring for, I'm all set," my father said.

"Although one of those movie popcorn poppers on wheels would be a nice addition, too."

"And then," John said, "we could turn the existing garage and the secret room into a two-story in-law apartment with a separate entrance for your dad, and we'd reconfigure the rest of the main house to make it work for us. Then we'd build a new garage with separate doors to each space."

"You do know this is insane," I said. "It would never work. And I have to tell you I don't appreciate you getting my father's hopes up like this."

My father pushed himself off the couch, stretched. "Well, that's enough fun and games for Homer and me tonight."

"What were you *thinking*?" I said to John once Homer had followed my father up the stairs and we were alone in the room.

"I think it's definitely worth sleeping on," John said.

Thirty-three

"Help," I said sometime in the middle of the night. "I'm stuck."

John's voice was raspy. "Do you mean stuck in old patterns or stuck in terms of making a decision?"

"I mean I'm freakin' stuck between the beds."

It should have been a dream, but I was really stuck. Even though I wasn't sure I was speaking to him, I must have rolled toward John in the middle of the night. The twin beds had separated and I ended up wedged between them, supported only by a hammock of bottom sheet that I could just feel was about to let loose at any moment.

Christine's old bed creaked as John got on his hands and knees and scooped me like a backhoe to the safety of my old bed.

"Thanks, Superman," I said.

I kissed him and he kissed me back, and even though we were both way too tired for this, one thing led to another.

"Shh," I said. "I cannot *believe* how much noise these springs make."

"Let's see if this helps." He rolled us over to the other bed, which was possibly even louder. Which completely cracked us both up. And then we weren't laughing anymore, and we stopped worrying about the noise, too. And everything else except how good it felt to be marooned together, just the two of us, making love in the dark.

"Boyohboy," I said when we were finished. "I needed that."

"You and me both." He slid one arm under my neck like a pillow, kissed me.

"Let's just stay like this forever," I said. "So we don't make any stupid mistakes."

"I'm not sure that's feasible. I'm actually feeling a slight numbness in this hand already."

"Sorry." I lifted up my head so he could retrieve his right arm. "You really don't think it would be totally insane to buy this house?"

"We've seen what's out there, Sarah. And it's such a grand old house."

"And my father has the potential to be such a grand old pain in the ass."

"Horatio would beg to disagree."

"Ha. This is true. My dad would definitely be a built-in dog sitter. But I still can't picture how we could get enough separation to make it work."

"What I was thinking is that we could break down the wall between this bedroom and the one next door with the bunk beds in it—"

"The boys' room."

"And that would give us plenty of space for a good size master with a walk-in closet and an en suite bathroom. And we'd still have two other bedrooms, one of which we could use for an office. And that room at the end that opens into that long screened-in balcony—"

"The sleeping porch."

"We could keep the sleeping porch, of course, and turn the adjoining room into a nice upstairs living space, so we'd have a place to get away to anytime we needed it."

"Which would be a lot," I said. "Possibly even constantly."

"So essentially, your dad would have one self-contained unit, and we'd have another. But the heart of the home could stay open, and we'd make it easily accessible to both units and to the rest of your family."

"If we did this, you do know my family would just stroll right up here anytime they felt like it, don't you?"

John yawned. "There's this new invention. It's called a lock. I think we should keep that beautiful center staircase intact, but we could close off the opening at the top of the stairs and put the entrance to our place there. And when we build the new garage, we could have stairs going up from that to our place, too. And if you think it's necessary, we could look into a moat as well."

I yawned, too. "Water won't stop them—they all took swimming lessons. And all those moat chemicals you have to put in to keep the water clear are such a pain. I was thinking more along the lines of barbed wire. You know, direct and to the point."

"Sure, or even a bucket of slime that falls on their heads when they try to pick our lock."

"I think a stun gun might be overkill," I said, "but maybe we could rig up some kind of boxing glove that's spring-released when you open our door."

John yawned again, like we were passing a single yawn back and forth between us. "I think it would make sense to finish your father's place first and get him moved in, then start the rest of it."

I tried to resist my turn to yawn, but I couldn't do it. "I have to tell you, I don't think I could sleep on these beds that long."

"So, we'll go out and buy a new bed tomorrow."

"Really? I never would have thought of that. You mean, we don't have to sleep on these torture racks just because they've been in this room forever?"

. . . . .

There was a nip in the air when I tiptoed out in my Winnie the Pooh slippers to feed the cat the next morning. It had been an unseasonably warm fall so far, but frost would definitely be on those pumpkins in no time.

The cat was already sitting on the edge of the patio, waiting for me.

"Where do you sleep?" I said. "Do you have a home but you just don't like what they feed you? Or do you need a bed? We're going out bed shopping today anyway."

The cat looked right at me with its green eyes, let out a piercing howl.

"Sorry," I said. I put the bowl down on the patio, pressed my back against the rough shingles of the house while it wolfed down every last bit of tuna.

I brought out the dog food and the water. The cat waited patiently for the Slim Jim-to-go and then took off.

I turned around to see my father and Horatio on the other side of the glass door.

"And how is our Miss Pebbles this fine morning?" my dad said.

"Sarah," I said.

My father laughed. "The cat, Sarry girl, the cat. Homer and I were all tuckered out, so I have to admit I'm a bit late getting her breakfast."

"You've been feeding her, too?"

"Yes indeedy, I have. Three squares a day, plus a Slim Jim or two when she meows for it. Our Miss Pebbles doesn't appear to be one of those gals that has to watch her figure. And don't you worry, she and Homer get along just fine as long as there's a door between them."

. . . . .

John and I were having a great time mattress shopping. We hopped from bed to bed in one of those mattress superstores where they make all the signs so confusing that you can't possibly compare mattress to mattress. We tried them all out anyway, like those dorky couples in the TV commercials.

"I wonder if we could get away with taking a short nap while we're here," I said.

"We could try it," John said, "but I think there might be some small print around here somewhere that says if you fall asleep on it, you own it."

Next we checked out a mattress boutique in the mall that had pretty much the same mattresses but with different names, and then we wandered through the mall so I could pick up a little gift for Siobhan.

We ended up taking a drive to Ikea, found a sleek king size bed frame and a latex mattress we both loved.

"I can't believe how comfortable this mattress is," I said.

John was scrolling through mattress reviews he'd pulled up on his phone. "Do you know that there are latex mattresses from the 1950s that are still in good shape?"

"That's nothing," I said. "The mattresses we've been sleeping on are probably older than that."

We stopped for lunch at a little place in a town where neither of us knew a soul.

"To us," I said as I raised my glass of seltzer.

"To us," John said. He touched his glass to mine.

We devoured our steak salads, which tasted so much better because someone else had made them.

I took a final bite, rested my fork on the edge of the plate.

"Okay," I said. "If we're crazy enough to do this, would that mean we won't ever have to go house hunting again?"

"Yes, it would. And you might have to dodge them at school, but other than that, it could also mean that we'll never have to see Nikki and Big Kevin again."

"Oh, you are so naïve," I said. "You have no idea what it's like to live in the 'burbs. There's nowhere to run, nowhere to hide. At one point or another, you see everyone again, usually when you just ran out for a minute to get something and you're wearing a T-shirt with stains on it and you forgot to brush your hair."

His Heath Bar eyes met mine. "Then we'll stay in. We'll pull up the drawbridge on our moat and barricade ourselves behind our new lock."

"And set the spring-released boxing glove?"

"Absolutely."

"Okay," I said. "I think I'm actually in."

· · · · ·

Siobhan was curled up on her bed in her turquoise terrycloth bathrobe, watching a movie on her laptop while she painted her toenails midnight blue.

"Hey," I said. "Great color."

"You can borrow it if you want when I'm done."

"Thanks. How're you feeling?"

"Okay. You know, crampy and I have this wicked backache. My mom said it's like back labor, so that's weird. Anyway, it sucks but it's not that bad."

"I'm really sorry for your loss," I said.

"Thanks," she said. "I'm really sorry for yours, too."

"Thanks," I said. "It would have been a great baby."

We were both crying, so I grabbed us each a tissue.

"I brought you something," I said. I reached into my purse, pulled out a little polka dot gift bag. "I should warn you though, you might think it's really lame."

Siobhan put the nail polish down on her bedside table, reached for the bag.

She pulled out the tissue paper, found the bracelet. It was silver and kind of retro, like one of the old ID bracelets that everybody used to wear a long, long time ago.

Siobhan read the initials I'd asked the jeweler to engrave on it. "N.D.?"

"No Dicks," I said. "Just in case you ever need a reminder."

CHAPTER

Thirty-four

The dining room table was dotted with so many white cardboard containers that it looked like we'd opened a takeout business.

"Rub-a-dub-dub, thanks for the grub, amen," my niece Lainie said.

"Yay, God," we all yelled.

Siobhan raised her glass along with the rest of us. She looked pale and sad, but she was here. And she was wearing the bracelet I'd given her.

"May the road rise up to meet you," my nephew Sean said.

"May the wind always be at your back," the rest of us yelled.

Our father stood up. "*I have spread my dreams under your feet;/ Tread softly because you tread on my dreams.*"

"Browning!" Christine said.

"No way," I said. "That's definitely Yeats."

"Show off," Christine said.

"It's not my fault you don't know your Yeats," I said.

"Behave, you two," our brother Johnny said. "Some of us like to enjoy our Sunday dinner in peace."

"Oh, grow up," Chris and I said at the same time.

"Owe me a coke," we both said.

"Sláinte!" everybody yelled.

His recitation cut short by his semi-adult children's bickering and the tantalizing smell of Chinese food, our dad leaned across the table and commandeered a container of pork-fried rice before he sat down again. We all followed his lead, grabbing the nearest takeout container, serving ourselves, passing it along to our right.

Horatio crawled under the kiddie section, positioning himself for a spill. Mother Teresa followed Horatio, but one of the rickety card tables was no match for her St. Bernard bulk. When it wobbled, the first glass of milk went over.

"And this is why," our father said, "your mother and I never let you kiddos have drinks at the table." He picked up his wine glass, took a long sip.

Since Mother Teresa was his dog, Michael jumped up and grabbed a handful of takeout napkins. His wife Phoebe jumped up to help, which we all knew meant their rocky marriage was in a good place right now.

I sipped my seltzer, dug into my Chinese food, hoped there might actually be leftovers after everybody finished chowing down. If so, one of the upsides of staying here was that John and I would get first dibs on them when we were hungry again in a couple hours, the downside of eating Chinese food.

We all stopped talking so we could focus on pigging out, and before we knew it we were passing around the pineapple chunks and the fortune cookies. Which pretty much did away with the quiet, since not only did our family believe that you had to choose your fortune cookie with your eyes closed for the fortune to come true, but you also had to read the fortune out loud and then eat the entire cookie.

A chorus of fortunes filled the air, the kids who couldn't read yet getting assistance from a cousin who could. *When you row another person across the river, you get there yourself. Two days from now, tomorrow will be yesterday. Things are not the way they seem. It could be better, but it's enough. Trust your intuition. You broke my cookie.*

"*The greatest risk is not taking one,*" I read.

"*Endurance and persistence will be rewarded,*" John read.

"*You will find a bushel of money,*" our father read. He pushed his chair back from the table and stood up. "You're probably wondering why I've gathered you all together today."

"Um," Michael said, "let's see. Because it's Sunday and basically we always eat here on Sundays?"

"We'll have no comments from the peanut gallery." My father raked his wayward clump of white hair out of his eyes, cleared his throat. "Hear ye, hear ye, I've made the executive decision to let Sarah and her fella build my man cavern."

"Great," Christine said. "I'm sure they'll do a really good job."

My father held up his hand. "Which I'll rent from them after they buy this house."

"*What?*" all five of my siblings said at once.

Nobody even bothered to add *owe me a Coke*.

"Siobhan," Carol said. "Why don't you take the kids into the family room and put on a movie for them."

"Sure," Siobhan said. "As long as you don't say anything else until I get back. I am so not missing this."

Billy Jr. crossed his arms over his chest. "I think we need to bring in an estate lawyer before we take this conversation any further."

"And a *real estate* lawyer, too," Carol said.

"Yeah, Dad," Johnny said. "I think it's crucial that we look at all the implications of this."

"This is our *inheritance* you're talking about," Christine said.

"Stop overreacting," I said. "It's not like we want the house for free. We're buying it."

"Fair market value?" Christine said.

"Fair market value given that Dad will be living here," I said.

"We'll need an appraisal," Billy Jr. said. "With the non-buying heirs choosing the appraiser."

Now I knew where that old saying about never mixing business with family had come from.

My father put two fingers in his mouth and let out the Hurlihy family whistle.

Once we'd all taken our hands off our ears, he continued. "This is how it's going to go down. I'll talk to my lawyer to make sure everything's on the up and up, and he'll keep it all in apple turnover order. If you don't like the lawyer I'm bankrolling, you can get your own second opinion, or overrule my choice and pick another one, in which case the legal beagle fee will be on your dime."

That pretty much quieted everybody down.

"So what John and I are going to do," I said, "is take out a mortgage to buy the house outright from Dad, and then we'll renovate it to make it work for all of us. Dad will deposit money from the sale, enough for rent for the next twenty years, into a bank account set up to automatically transfer the money to us on the first of the month. If he's still alive and kicking after twenty years, he gets to live here rent free."

"Now that's what I call motivation," our father said. "I'm going for the hundred-and-one club. And I expect you kiddos to throw me one helluva big birthday bash if I make it. Balloons and everything."

"And," I said, "if at any point Dad decides he wants to move out, he gets to keep whatever's left in the bank account."

"What if he dies?" Carol said.

"Bite your tongue," our father said.

"If he dies," I said, "the rent money goes into the pool with the rest of Dad's assets."

"What about the furniture?" Christine said. "It's so not fair that you get to keep it all."

"We're leaving most of the downstairs as shared space," I said. "But our new bed is being delivered Tuesday, so if anybody wants any of the upstairs furniture or anything on the walls, including posters of teenage heart throbs, get it out of here by the end of next week."

"Don't touch my bed yet," our father said. "But if you play your cards right, you might get a shot at it down the road. Homer and I are considering a round bed for my man cavern. We hear the ladies love them."

"Not to be rude," Christine said, "but I'd like to point out that Sarah doesn't exactly have a stellar track record as far as relationships go. And the two of you aren't even married. What happens if you break up?"

"Thanks," I said.

"I've got a marriage proposal on the table," John said. "Sarah just wants to take this one step at a time."

Billy Jr.'s arms were still crossed over his chest. "Are you willing to sign a prenup?" he said.

"Whatever it takes," John said. "I'm all in, and I'm not going anywhere."

"Enough," our dad said. "Never let it be said that your father doesn't keep things fair and square, so I'm going to give you kiddos one chance to turn it all around. Anybody who'd like to buy this house instead can make their best offer now. If we end up in a bidding war, so be it."

A few of my siblings made eye contact with their spouses, but nobody said anything.

"Once . . ." my father said. "Twice . . . Thrice . . . "

"Speak now or forever hold your peace," he added.

He held one hand up over his head like a gavel.

"Sold!" he yelled as pounded his fist on the dining room table. "And if any of you kiddos don't like it, you can ship up or shape out."

CHAPTER

Thirty-five

My father and Horatio had taken the ice cream truck out to make an après dinner Bark & Roll Forever run, so John and I had the house to ourselves.

"Well, that went well," John said, "all things considered. At least I think it did. I have to admit that I sometimes have a hard time telling when it comes to your family."

"It went really well," I said. "Other than the fact that they left us with the cleanup."

"But we got the leftovers."

"This is true," I said. "And it looks like they're going to clear out most of the upstairs furniture, too." I closed the ancient dishwasher, put my arms around John. "Are you sure you want to do this?"

"Absolutely," he said.

We kissed on it.

"We are now certifiably bat shit crazy," I said when we came up for air.

"Come on," he said, "let's go walk our forty acres-to-be before it's too dark to see them."

"I hate to break it to you," I said, "but there's only about an acre and a half. But sure, just give me a minute to powder my nose first."

"Now *that's* funny," John said.

I climbed the creaky stairs to the upstairs bathroom. I checked out the gallery of photos as I always did, remembered that I still hadn't added a photo of John and me.

Like so many things in life, I knew it before I really knew it. But that didn't make finding the irrefutable proof that I wasn't pregnant any easier to take. I closed my eyes as the disappointment hit me. In a family that bred like rabbits, why did even this have to be so hard for me?

I opened the bathroom closet. Way in the back of a shelf I found an orange and blue-striped tampon box that had to be from the '80s. I flashed back to a tampon TV commercial from around the same time that had done as much to mess me up as anything else during my teenage years. A perfect blond girl windsurfing, the orange and blue of the sail matching the stripes of the tampon box exactly. Another perfect blond girl riding horseback. And still another perfect blond girl doing something else, maybe walking the beach. They were all dressed in crisp clean white, the point being they weren't the least bit worried about either their tampons or their lives letting them down.

I sighed, hoped I wouldn't get toxic shock syndrome from using a tampon that had been stored in a closet for decades.

John was waiting for me at the foot of the stairs. The massive oak front door creaked as he opened it. We made a loop around the yard, our arms wrapped around each other, talking about the best place to put the new garage, how great it would be when our new bed was delivered.

The temperature was dropping quickly as dusk closed in on us, but we sat for a moment on the cold metal seat of the porch swing anyway.

"So," I said. "We're not pregnant."

John put his arm around me. "I'm sorry."

"Yeah. Me, too."

The calico cat appeared at the base of the leafless Japanese maple like a vision. Her piercing green eyes met mine.

"Pebbles," I said.

I was just about to introduce her to John when a tiny kitten, its orange and white fur covered with dirt, toddled out from beneath the porch. Pebbles sprinted over and head-butted it back under the porch, gave me another piercing look.

John was already on his feet, trying to look between the porch boards.

"Did you see that?" he said. "I think we've got a litter of kittens under here. No wonder Horatio goes nuts whenever we bring him in this way."

Another kitten, this one black and white and dirty all over, poked its head out from under the porch. Pebbles nudged it back under and followed it.

John pulled his key ring out of his pocket, turned on a tiny laser flashlight attached to it. "I think I see three of them, maybe four." He got down on his hands and knees, his nose practically touching the porch as he peered between the boards.

I got down on my hands and knees next to John, tried to count the blurs of fur making a beeline for Pebbles in the cave-like darkness.

"We need to get them inside so they don't freeze to death," John said. "How about if you go get them some food and water while I Google up the best way to do it?"

I got back up on my feet again as I had so many times before. On the one hand, my life being my life, leave it to the universe to absolutely surround me with babies and then give me a litter of kittens instead.

But on the other hand, *ohmigod*, they were soooo cute.

. . . .

Stay tuned for *Must Love Dogs: Who Let the Cats In?*, Book 5 of the *Must Love Dogs* series!

Claire

Thanks so much for reading *Must Love Dogs: Bark & Roll Forever*, book four of the *Must Love Dogs* series. I hope you enjoyed it! Reviews are becoming more and more important in helping readers discover books, so I'd really appreciate it if you'd take the time to write a short review or tell a friend you've just finished reading it. Thank you for your support!

I've included an excerpt of *Seven Year Switch*, which has just been released in a new edition. Happy reading!

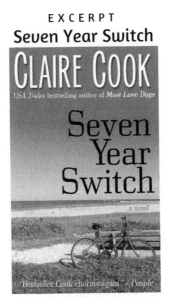

"[A] beach chair worthy read."—*New York Times*

"[A] hot summer beach book."—*USA Today*

"Bestseller Cook charms again in this lively, warm-hearted look at changing courses mid-life."—*People*

"A beach tote couldn't ask for more."—*Kirkus Reviews*

"Roll out your beach blanket for this sweet summer read about making mistakes and moving on."
—*Publishers Weekly*

CHAPTER ONE

I sailed into the community center just in time to take my Lunch Around the World class to China. I hated to be late, but my daughter Anastasia had forgotten part of her school project.

"Oh, honey," I'd said when she called from the school office. "Can't it wait till tomorrow? I'm just leaving for work." I tried not to wallow in it, but sometimes the logistics of being a single mom were pretty exhausting.

"Mom," she whispered, "it's a diorama of a cow's habitat, and I forgot the *cow.*"

I remembered seeing the small plastic cow grazing next to Anastasia's cereal bowl at breakfast, but how it had meandered into the dishwasher was anyone's guess. I gave it a quick rinse under the faucet and let it air-dry on the ride to school. From there I hightailed it to the community center.

Though it wasn't the most challenging part of my work week, this Monday noon-to-two-o'clock class got me home before my daughter, which in the dictionary of my life made it the best kind of gig. Sometimes I even had time for a cup of tea before her school bus came rolling down the street. Who knew a cup of tea could be the most decadent part of your day.

I plopped my supplies on the kitchen counter and jumped right in. "In Chinese cooking, it's important to balance colors as well as contrasts in tastes and textures."

"Take a deep breath, honey," one of my favorite students said. Her name was Ethel, and she had bright orange lips and *I Love Lucy* hair. "We're not going anywhere."

A man with white hair and matching eyebrows started singing "On a Slow Boat to China." A couple of the women giggled. I took that deep breath.

" *Yum cha* is one of the best ways to experience this," I continued. "Literally, *yum cha* means 'drinking tea,' but it actually encompasses both the tea drinking and the eating of dim sum, a wide range of light dishes served in small portions."

"Yum-yum," a man named Tom said. His thick glasses were smudged with fingerprints, and he was wearing a T-shirt that said TUNE IN TOMORROW FOR A DIFFERENT SHIRT.

"Let's hope," I said. "In any case, *dim sum* has many translations: 'small eats,' of course, but also 'heart's delight,' 'to touch your heart,' and even 'small piece of heart.' I've often wondered if Janis Joplin decided to sing the song she made famous after a dim sum experience."

Last night when I was planning my lesson, this had seemed like a brilliant and totally original cross-cultural connection, but everybody just nodded politely.

We made dumplings and pot stickers and mini spring rolls, and then we moved on to fortune cookies. Custard tarts or even mango pudding would have been more culturally accurate, but fortune cookies were always a crowd-pleaser. I explained that the crispy, sage-laced cookies had actually been invented in San Francisco, and tried to justify my choice by adding that the original inspiration for fortune cookies possibly dated back to the thirteenth century, when Chinese soldiers slipped rice paper messages into mooncakes to help coordinate their defense against Mongolian invaders.

Last night Anastasia had helped me cut small strips of white paper to write the fortunes on. And because the cookies had to be wrapped around the paper as soon as they came out of the oven, while they were still pliable, I'd bought packages of white cotton gloves at CVS and handed out one to each person. The single gloves kept the students' hands from burning and were less awkward than using pot holders.

They also made the class look like aging Michael Jackson impersonators. A couple of the women started to sing "Beat It" while they stirred the batter, and then everybody else joined in. There wasn't a decent singer in the group, but some of them could still remember how to moonwalk.

After we finished packing up some to take home, we'd each placed one of our cookies in a big bamboo salad bowl. There'd been more giggling as we passed the bowl around the long, wobbly wooden table and took turns choosing a cookie and reading the fortune, written by an anonymous classmate, out loud.

"*The time is right to make new friends.*"

"*A great adventure is in your near future.*"

"*A tall dark-haired man will come into your life.*"

" *You will step on the soil of many countries, so don't forget to pack clean socks.*"

"*The one you love is closer than you think,*" Ethel read. Her black velour sweat suit was dusted with flour.

"Oo-ooh," the two friends taking the class with her said. One of them elbowed her.

The fortune cookies were a hit. So what if my students seemed more interested in the food than in its cultural origins. I wondered if they'd still have signed up if I'd shortened the name of the class from Lunch Around the World to just plain Lunch. My class had been growing all session, and not a single person had asked for a refund. In this economy, everybody was cutting everything, and even community center classes weren't immune. The best way to stay off the chopping block was to keep your classes full and your students happy.

I reached over and picked up the final fortune cookie, then looked at my watch. "Oops," I said. "Looks like we're out of time." I stood and smiled at the group. "Okay, everybody, that's it for today." I nodded at the take-out cartons I'd talked the guy at the Imperial Dragon into donating to the cause. "Don't forget your cookies, and remember, next week we'll be lunching in Mexico." I took care to pronounce it *Mehico*.

"Tacos?" T-shirt Tom asked.

"You'll have to wait and see-eee," I said, mostly because I hadn't begun to think about next week. Surviving this one was enough of a challenge.

"Not even a hint?" a woman named Donna said.

I shook my head and smiled some more.

They took their time saying thanks and see you next week as they grabbed their take-out boxes by the metal handles and headed out the door. A few even offered to help me pack up, but I said I was all set. It was faster to do it myself.

As I gave the counters a final scrub, I reviewed the day's class in my head. Overall, I thought it had gone well, but I still didn't understand why the Janis Joplin reference had fallen flat.

I put the sponge down, picked up a wooden spoon, and got ready to belt out "Piece of My Heart."

When I opened my mouth, a chill danced the full length of my spine. I looked up. A man was standing just outside the doorway. He had dark, wavy hair cascading almost to his shoulders and pale, freckled skin. He was tall and a little too thin. His long fingers gripped the doorframe, as if a strong wind might blow him back down the hallway.

He was wearing faded jeans and the deep green embroidered Guatemalan shirt I'd given my husband just before he abandoned us seven years ago.

No. Way.

I'd dreamed this scene a thousand times, played it out hundreds of different ways.

I'd kissed him and killed him over and over and over again, violently and passionately, and at every emotional stop in between.

"Jill?" he said.

My mouth didn't seem to be working. *That's my name, don't wear it out* popped into my head randomly, as if to prove my brain wasn't firing on all cylinders either.

"Can I talk to you for a minute?" he said.

My heart leaped into action and my hands began to shake, but other than that, I couldn't feel a thing. I remembered reading that in a fight-or-flight reaction, deep thought shuts down and more primitive responses take over.

I picked up the bowl. I gulped down some air. I measured the distance between us. I tried to imagine my feet propelling me past him—out of the building, into my car, safely back home. Flight was winning by a landslide.

"No," I said. "Actually, you can't."

He followed me out to my car, keeping a safe distance. I clicked the lock and balanced the bowl on my left hip while I opened the door of my battered old Toyota.

"How is she?" he asked. "How's Asia?"

"Her *name* is Anastasia," I said.

But the damage had been done. In one nickname, four letters, he'd brought it all back. We'd spent much of my pregnancy tracing our family trees online, looking for the perfect name for our daughter-to-be. In a sea of Sarahs and Claras and Helens, Anastasia jumped right out, a long-forgotten relative on Seth's side of the family. Since we didn't have any details, we made up our own. Our daughter would be Anastasia, the lost princess of Russia. Sometimes she'd have escaped the revolution only to be frozen to wait for the perfect parents to be born. Other times she came to us via simple reincarnation. We'd curled up on our shabby couch in front of our hand-me-down TV and watched the animated *Anastasia* over and over again, until we could do most of the voice-overs right along with Meg Ryan and John Cusack.

When she was born, Anastasia brought her own twist to the story. From a combined ethnic pool swimming with ancestors from Ireland, England, Scotland, Italy, and Portugal, she'd somehow inherited the most amazing silky straight dark hair and exotic almond-shaped eyes. We nicknamed her Asia, a continent we loved, the place we'd met.

I closed my eyes. "She's ten," I said. "She's fine. I'm fine. Leave us alone, Seth. Just leave us the hell alone."

By the time I opened my eyes, he was already walking away.

It wasn't until I went to put my hands on the steering wheel that I realized I was still holding my fortune cookie. It had shattered into pieces, and the thin strip of paper inside had morphed into a crumb-and-sweat-covered ball. I peeled it off my palm.

Something you lost will soon show up.

"Thanks for the warning," I said.

. . . . .

Keep reading! Order your copy of the *Seven Year Switch* paperback or download the ebook.

ACKNOWLEDGMENTS

On May 1, 2000, my first novel was published. On May 1, 2015, exactly fifteen years later, I hit the *New York Times* bestseller list for the very first time. When you do the work you love and have incredible readers supporting you, it is never, EVER too late! A huge thank you to each and every one of you for reading my books and spreading the word. I never forget for a moment that you give me the gift of this career. Love you all!

A huge alphabetical thank you to Ken Harvey, Beth Hoffman, and Jack and Pam Kramer, for their sharp eyes and huge hearts. I SO couldn't have done it without you!

Forever thanks to Jake, Garet and Kaden for always being there.

ABOUT CLAIRE

I wrote my first novel in my minivan at 45. At 50, I walked the red carpet at the Hollywood premiere of the adaptation of my second novel, *Must Love Dogs*, starring Diane Lane and John Cusack. I'm now the *New York Times* bestselling author of 14 books. If you have a buried dream, take it from me, it is NEVER too late!

I've reinvented myself once again by turning *Must Love Dogs* into a series and writing my first nonfiction book, *Never Too Late: Your Roadmap to Reinvention (without getting lost along the way)*, in which I share everything I've learned on my own journey that might help you in yours. I've also become a reinvention speaker, so if you know anyone who's looking for a fun and inspiring speaker, I hope you'll send them to http://ClaireCook.com/speaking/. Thanks!

I was born in Virginia, and lived for many years in Scituate, Massachusetts, a beach town between Boston and Cape Cod. My husband and I have recently moved to the suburbs of Atlanta to be closer to our two adult kids, who actually want us around again!

I have the world's most fabulous readers and I'm forever grateful to all of you for giving me the gift of this career. Midlife Rocks!

xxxxxClaire

HANG OUT WITH ME!
ClaireCook.com
Facebook.com/ClaireCookauthorpage
Twitter.com/ClaireCookwrite
Pinterest.com/ClaireCookwrite

Be the first to find out when my next book comes out and stay in the loop for giveaways and insider excerpts: ClaireCook.com/newsletter.

Made in the USA
San Bernardino, CA
20 June 2017